D0758746

DATE			

JEWEL
OF THE
MOON

JEWEL
OF THE
MOON

Short Stories by
William Kotzwinkle

G. P. Putnam's Sons   *New York*

G. P. Putnam's Sons
Publishers Since 1838
200 Madison Avenue
New York, NY 10016

Library of Congress Cataloging-in-Publication Data

Kotzwinkle, William.
Jewel of the moon.

I. Title.
PS3561.085J4   1985   813'.54   85-19254
ISBN 0-399-13113-2

Printed in the United States of America
1   2   3   4   5   6   7   8   9   10

Contents

The Day Stokowski Saved the World

The One-man Band of 14th Street had no legs. Where his knees should have been were two leather pads, which allowed him to go forward on his stumps, in short slow steps. Around his neck was hung a small bass drum, which he beat with a stick held in his right hand. In his left hand was a gourd full of seeds, which he shook in rhythm with the incessant beat of his drum.

To the top of the drum was fastened a cymbal, played through a system of levers attached to his left stump, so that as he walked the cymbal halves parted automatically, and came together again with a constant clanging. As he walked and played, he sang the words of a never-changing song:

Long way 'cross town

His black face was wreathed in smiles as he moved through the crowd of shoppers. His closeness to the pavement gave him the appearance of great stability, like a weighted plastic clown which always bounces back standing, no matter how hard it is struck. He never paused a step, except at stoplights, and his music swelled stronger in those pauses:

> *Bump! Clang! Shika-shika*
> *Long way 'cross town*
> *Bump! Clang! Shika-shika*

Uptown, on a similar musical pilgrimage to nowhere, was another black man, with the same amputation and vocation. His stumps were fitted inside an orange crate which was mounted on planks supported by roller skate wheels. A toy trumpet was fastened to the top of the orange crate, close to his lips. With his right hand he played a toy piano set inside the crate between his stumps. His left hand struck a toy drum attached to the side of the crate. He pushed himself along, or let himself be pushed, an American flag waving from the front of his low-slung vehicle.

He rode all morning, as far downtown as fortune carried him, a drifter in the tide of Broadway, singing his own incessant song:

> *Columbus the Jim of the Ocean*

Two boys from Hell's Kitchen who were hanging around Times Square decided to take him on tour. They pushed him along, far downtown, past 42nd Street, and on down through the 30's, the 20's, through Chelsea into the teens.

Through the stinking heat of the summer day, above the roar of traffic, a shopper on the corner of 14th Street and 7th Avenue could hear strange and diverse melodies approaching:

Bump! Clang! Shika-shika
Long way 'cross town
Shika-shika

Fraaaaak! Plinka-plinka
Columbus the Jim of the Ocean
Plinka-plinka, fraaaaaack!

Down 7th Avenue came the Orange-crate Man, shaking his head and singing, striking his toy piano, blowing his toy trumpet. Across 7th Avenue came the One-man Band of 14th Street, stumping along, walloping his drum. Suddenly their eyes met. Simultaneously, their music ceased. Despite the roar of buses, trucks, and taxis, a strange silence seemed to pervade the intersection. The One-man Band dropped his drumstick to his side, his smile gone and, with it, the wild, almost insane confidence one always saw in his eyes as he crossed town, marching on his stumps.

The Orange-crate Man leaned forward, peering across the street. His face too had lost its powerful grin, by which he was known up and down Broadway, and the

Hell's Kitchen boys seemed caught up in his sudden shock, for they stood unmoving, like figures frozen in a dream.

The shoppers, the drivers, moved along, following the changing color of the traffic lights, but the two amputees did not move. Each was staring at a mirror image of himself—a foreshortened black man hung with toy instruments. A moment ago they were the life and joy of 7th Avenue and 14th Street, musical giants, their song the perfect expression of great and tenacious hearts— now they were stumpy beggars, afraid to make a sound, embarrassed and ashamed.

The light changed and changed again. The legless statues did not move. Their drumming song was forgotten, that drum and song which had come to them somewhere in the past, to lead them out of the stagnating gloom of an amputee ward, or from a stifling Manhattan room, into the streets, clanging with music, flag waving, reborn!

Now they floundered. A woman shopper stopped and asked the One-man Band if he was alright. The little fellow did not look at her. Across the street the Hell's Kitchen boys asked the Orange-crate Man where he wanted to go, but he did not answer. The awful moment of amputation had come again, like a shark out of the sea. The full and terrible reality of their loss was on them, as sometimes we remember lost loved ones, with a sorrow that continues to overwhelm if it is looked at a moment too long. Now they looked, now they saw clearly; now, as once before, when their legs had been seized in the jaws of a wretched destiny and the pain was too great to bear, they fled into numbing isolation.

Riding the crosstown bus at that hour was a mentally retarded delivery man, short, ill-proportioned, wearing directly on the center of his head a hat two sizes too small. Through his idiot's eyes, which gazed at the world with constant surprise as if it were a place forever strange, he recognized his stop—7th Avenue and 14th Street.

He rose up and went to the door. As the bus stopped he descended, to his own music. He was a whistler, but not the ordinary absent-minded street whistler. His whistling was a thinly conscious thread, an incomplete scale whistled over and over like the song of the brain-fever bird of the jungles, and it was all that kept him from plunging over the edge of the world into incomprehensible night.

His lips were huge, blown out and swollen from his constant pursing of them, and he struck the sidewalk, whistling, directly in the midst of the deep silence of the black amputees. He looked around, still whistling his intense symphony. Familiar with the music of the abyss, he saw clearly as Stokowski that the inner tempo of existence was threatened, for two of the musicians had forgotten the score, and to forget the score was to lose all to chaos. Entering 7th Avenue, directly between the two singers, he raised his hand as if to stop traffic, and signaled the downbeat with unmistakable authority.

Their music leapt out of them, shot out of their being,

exactly in time, perfectly together, blended with the idiot-whistler's tune:

> *Bump! Fraaaak! Tweeet*
> *Long way Columbus*
> *Clang! Shika-plinka Tweet Tweet*
> *Cross Jim of the Ocean town Tweet*

The idiot delivery man moved on with his package. The Hell's Kitchen kids turned their maestro around, pushing him back uptown toward 42nd Street. The One-man Band of 14th Street moved on, smiling westward toward the sea.

The Curio Shop

"Now here, sir, is a lovely and might I say traditional example . . ." The Seller pointed a finger at the decorative sphere, set against a deep velvet cloth.

The Collector leaned on the edge of the counter and studied the bauble. Its workmanship might be good but it was hard to tell, owing to large sooty stains on its surface and, beneath that, what appeared to be rust, or some fatal corrosion which had permanently marred the interior.

"I'll let you have it cheap," said the Seller, spying the critical look of the Collector. Business wasn't good; the shop was seldom visited anymore.

"Is it—" The Collector touched at it with his monocle, studying the piece more closely. "—still enchanted?"

"The occasional wail, sir. You know the phenomenon, I'm sure."

"The true spirit, or merely an echo?"

The Seller sighed. He couldn't misrepresent the piece. He'd like to, naturally. He needed the sale. But he couldn't afford to offend a good customer. "It no longer contains a true spirit, sir, I regret to say."

The Collector nodded, turning the bauble slightly with the edge of his monocle.

"But—" continued the Seller, a trifle urgently, "—the echo is authentic, sir."

"I'm sure," said the Collector, with a sideways glance, his eyes showing only a momentary flicker of contempt.

"Well, sir," said the Seller, defending himself against the glance, "there are clever copies in existence. The ordinary collector can be deceived. Not that you, sir—" He hastened to correct himself. "—are an ordinary collector."

"Happy that you think so." The Collector twisted the ball in his hands, examining the portions of the surface not corrupted by time and bad handling. It was shameful the way certain pieces deteriorated. But the work was authentic, he didn't need the Seller to tell him that. You could see the little original touches all over the object, though they were badly encrusted. Unfortunately you couldn't clean the damn things, no matter how you worked at them; once the corrosion began it couldn't be reversed. He wondered sometimes why he bothered with them at all. But then, it was always amusing when company came and one had a new piece to show. He could have it put in a gold mount; that'd show it off to better advantage. Or hang it from a chain in his study, where the lighting was usually muted and the defects of the sphere wouldn't show too badly.

"Let me . . . please, sir . . ." The Seller pulled out a cloth from his pocket, attempted to shine the tiny patch of transparency on the ball. But as the cloth touched it, the wailing came forth, long, low, and chilling; echo or not, it went right through the Seller's soul.

"The echo is fresh," said the Collector, smiling for the first time. "The spirit must have departed only recently."

"So I'm told, sir." The Seller resumed his bit of dusting on the surface, more confident now, for he'd seen the smile and knew he had a sale. "That's precisely what the Caravan Master said when I bought it from him, sir—the spirit has but recently departed."

The Collector squinted through his glass, savoring the moment, knowing the piece must be his, for the wail was strong; he could listen to it at his leisure, and learn the story of the bauble, who had made it and when. All that would still be in the echo. Pity the true spirit had fled—that would have been a find!

"Well, I suppose I'll have to have this," he said. "My wife will hate it, of course."

"Because of the wailing, sir?"

"Puts her off. Gives her the creeps."

"I must admit—" The Seller continued his dusting. "—it gives me the creeps, too."

"You don't know how to listen," said the Collector. "You must get past the superficial sound, and hear the traces of its inner voice."

"You have the knack for it, sir, that's clear." The

Seller masked his disdain behind a cheerful smile. He'd be glad to have the cursed thing out of the shop, and be done with its bloody wailing.

"Much to be learned, much," said the Collector, aware that he was revealing too great an excitement, and knowing he'd suffer in the bargain, but he didn't care at this point. The wailing had thrilled him. These little ornaments were filled with surprises, always, even when they were as old as this one, and all that remained of their past glory was a fading echo.

"Microbes," he said, inspecting the ball with his glass again. "They say that's what causes the deterioration."

"I've heard the same, sir. Tiny organisms that feed upon the workings."

"Once," said the Collector, holding the ball up to the light, "it was brand-new. Can we ever conceive of the beauty it must have contained? How splendid its workmanship? Eh?"

"If you'll examine that bit of transparency, sir—"

"My good man," said the Collector, ignoring the Seller's suggestion, "if the spirit that once inhabited this ball were still in it, it could tell us more than just who made it and when—" He paused, his eyes shining with the intoxication of the connoisseur. "—it would engage us in deep discussion, would whisper to us of the wondrous workings of its mechanisms, give us the secret of its maker, would grant us, in short, the favor of its enchanting company, but—" He placed the ball back on its dark velvet cloth. "—this is a lifeless trinket now."

The Seller concealed a sneer behind his polishing

cloth. These collectors were such pompous old bores; listening to their twaddle made him sick. "You saw my sale sign, sir. Fifty percent off all items in the shop."

"Yes," said the Collector, disappointed at his failure to kindle true appreciation in the Seller. But what did these merchants know of subtlety? And in any case, once he was home, and visitors came, then he could expand fully, then he'd have his fun, in the comfort of his armchair in the study, with the fire crackling and the bauble suspended on a suitable chain, in the shadows by the window, perhaps. "All right, how much do you want for it?"

"As you can see, sir, through this bit of transparency, the center is filled with jewels—"

"But surely that's not unusual—"

"The fakes, sir, are glass-filled—"

* * *

The Collector adjusted his top hat, turned up the collar on his cape. The bauble was in his pocket, and a thin smile played upon his lips. He'd driven a hard and cunning bargain.

The Seller graciously held the door, sly satisfaction in his eyes. He'd gotten twice what the trinket was worth. These foreign collectors often think they know it all.

"Do you remember, perchance," asked the Collector, drawing the bauble from his pocket as he stepped into the bright street, "what the Caravan Master called this thing when he sold it to you?"

"A peculiar name, sir," replied the Seller. "He called it Earth."

"Earth. I see. Very well then, my good man, I shall undoubtedly visit you again."

"My pleasure, sir, always."

The Seller closed his door, and watched through the window as the Collector walked on down the glittering milky boulevard.

Jewel of the Moon

She and Mother watched through the curtains as the handsome stranger and Father discussed her marriage. The stranger offered money, which Father said was too little. Then they smoked and Father grew poetic, calling her Jewel of the Moon, and she was afraid the bargaining would never finish. She desperately hoped it would, for the stranger was fine-looking and the frog-faced rug-seller of the village was also seeking her hand. Take me away, whispered her heart, and perhaps the stranger felt its delicate beat, for he suddenly doubled his offer of gold and Father agreed.

On the day of their marriage a celebration was held in the village. The drums spoke their hollow song, she danced, the sun was bright. Then as afternoon grew late, he took her away, onto the country road, toward his own village.

Confused, frightened, delighted, mad with anxiety, a virgin, she did not know what to say to him, though her thighs spoke silken words through her gown as she walked along the dirt road, aflame.

The setting sun cast her husband's face in deep red. His eyes burned through her and she too grew red, her stomach flip-flopping, young and silly, but her breasts were moving sweetly as she walked, her hips were full and swayed and how pretty were her bare painted toes. Her ears dangled with earrings and through their jingling she heard the sound of a distant flute.

"That is the musician of my village, welcoming you," said her husband.

She fell into sadness. To strange music, into a strange town, with childhood gone, Jewel of the Moon is letting herself be led. But circling, dancing in the air, the song enticed her, set her dreaming. Soon she would let her black hair down.

Ahead she saw the trees and rooftops of his village, and doubt ruined her again. Afraid to look at him now, she pulled her veil over her head, to hide, to die. How cruel of Father to abandon her, to trade Jewel of the Moon for two bags of gold to this stranger.

"Here we are," he said, turning onto a narrow dirt path.

At the end of the path she saw a small house. Slowly she walked toward it, numb with fear. Still she kept dignity, which Mother had taught her to maintain always, whatever the situation. She did not slouch, tremble, or faint crossing the strange threshold to the cool gloom of the living room. Out of the corner of her eye, through a small doorway, she saw the rattan foot of a bed.

Her husband pointed toward that room and she walked to the doorway, heart thundering.

A purple lamp hung there, and her skin turned to pale moon shades as she walked through the opening. My husband is an exotic, she thought, inspecting the ornate shade of the lamp, on which a thousand-armed God was embracing his naked purple-skinned wife. Will I be sophisticated or will I scream? In the purple den of love, she turned to face him.

He unwrapped the white marriage turban from his head and dark hair fell to his shoulders. Tenderness? Or will he ravish me with bloody sword? Her body played possibilities as he lit incense on the tiny altar by the bed.

She looked down at her toes, wanting to conceal the rest of herself from him, wanting also to reveal what he hadn't seen, wanting this and wanting that, frozen flame in a purple place. The window was near and she could escape, but she longed to surprise him with the fullness of her thighs.

"Sit down," he said. She sat on the edge of the bed, dropping her hips into the soft embrace of the mattress. I am ready.

He knelt before her, looked into her eyes. This is the moment.

"I'll sleep down here," he said, stretching himself out on the floor at her feet.

I must awake, she thought, trying to escape the silly dream.

"Perhaps you would like a glass of milk with a piece of toast?" he asked, raising himself on one elbow.

She looked dumbly at the far wall of the bedroom, as her husband hustled off to the kitchen. Nervously, she opened the ribbon on her hair and let her long black head-cloak fall, scented and shimmering. I am Jewel of the Moon. Why does he talk of milk and toast?

"Here I am," he said, coming toward her on his knees, holding the milk and toast.

She took the plate. He turned back down at her feet. "Just kick me if you want anything else."

I have married a madman. Jewel of the Moon peered over the edge of the bed.

Her husband's eyes quickly opened. "Anything else, Perfect One?"

Unable to speak, she shook her head, and though she was not hungry she ate the toast. Then she stretched out on the wedding bed and stared at the ceiling. I must escape. She waited until she was sure he was asleep, but as soon as her foot touched the floor, he was up, like a watchdog, watching her.

Frightened, she lay back down. She would look for another chance, but sleep overtook her, and she spent the night dreaming of a powerful horse who galloped her to freedom.

*   *   *

"Here is your breakfast, Daughter of the Sun," said her ridiculous husband in the morning, coming toward her on his knees with a silver tray of food.

She ate and he sat at her feet, watching the window, heedless of her morning beauty, as if his fearful bargaining for her had never been. She was truly miserable, for it was real, had been no dream, she'd married an imbecile. *That is what he looks like, sitting there. He looks like an incredible idiot and I hate him.*

"Here," she said, contemptuously, "I'm done."

"At once." Taking away her cup and plate, he scurried off to the kitchen. She watched him return, to the doorway only, where he lay down, and she covered her tearful eyes. Peeking through her fingers she saw him lying there, doglike, eyes on her, bright, stupid. *She wanted to wave her tail at him, give him something to growl about.*

"I'm going for a walk," she said, defiantly stepping over the crumpled man on the floor. *Perhaps he will bite me, seek to hold me somehow.*

"I'll just walk a few paces behind you," he said. "If you want anything, just spit on me."

They walked through the streets of his strange village. She knew no one there, except the shadowy dog at her heels. He lapped along behind her to the well. Women were fetching water and they gave her inquiring looks, as her husband curled up at her feet in the sand. *They know I've been tricked by a weak-kneed fiend.* Looking down she wanted to spit on him, but the women would love that too much.

She left the well and walked on through the village, curling her toes in the hot sand as the men of this new village eyed her bare feet and a bit more, perhaps, for her hips were expressing themselves, too enthusiastically for a married woman, but her so-called husband was licking along at the ground. I'll give him one more chance this afternoon.

*   *   *

She sat upon the bed, brushing her long hair over her heart. Her ankles were smooth and bare and she wriggled her toes as he entered the room, bathed in the gold of afternoon. But there came no spicy kiss upon her toes, only curried peas, served on a tray which he placed on her thighs.

*   *   *

Night. Beneath purple light he gave her milk and toast and curled down again on the floor. The milk and toast made her brain sleepy, but her pale thighs wanted something indescribably nice, and it wasn't milk toast.

She tossed on her pillow, recalling the passages from the Holy Sutra on Love. I studied the book faithfully, yet here I am, perspiring on an empty bed. She rose up and with her bare foot gave her husband a kick.

He rolled over, looking up from the floor like a whipped mongrel.

"Stop snoring," she said, angrily.

"I will stop breathing," he said, and wrapped a strip of linen around his nose.

The moon crossed her pillow. Slowly her passion subsided, like a body fallen away, and she moved in dreams, a queen with many servants, all of them her idiot husband.

* * *

As the wedding month went by, she grew tense. Her husband was silent, devoted, treated her like a queen, and she loathed him and his entire line of ancestors. She thrust her foot out, so that he might remove her sandals, which he did, handling her foot as carefully as a dish of precious rice, except that he did not taste or swallow the delight and it soon grew cold.

She raised her feet on the barren marriage bed, drawing her knees up to her breasts. I am so young. There are other men. They would not treat me like this. They would torture me with glances, drive me mad with their eyes. I will die soon of dullness. Neglect can end woman's life, so says the Holy Sutra.

She felt the end of the mattress suddenly sink down with unusual force. "What are you doing?" she cried, for the impudent servant was sitting on the foot of the bed.

"If you want anything," he said, curling up at her feet, "just kick me in the face."

She pulled herself into a fetal ball, wishing she could be reborn in some hidden world. The night bird blew his flute, she lay in purple moon-robe, and dreams of mating came to her. A shining man held her, ghostly thin he was, and she stretched herself out beneath him, at the same time touching with her toe accidentally the face of the vile sleeper at her feet.

"Yes, Tower of Grace," said her husband sitting up quickly, "have you bad dreams? I will make a cup of tea which relaxes the mind."

He left and returned with a silver tray, surrounded by steam. He poured the tea and she let the sheet fall away from her, moonlight coming on her breasts, bare behind her thin midnight gown.

"This will help," he said, handing her a cup of the tea, not even glancing at the pale cups she had so immodestly revealed. She drew the sheet around herself again, hating him, and drank the tea, a gentle herb, which soon brought the charm of sleep.

Each night, following milk and toast, he slipped onto the foot of the bed, like a dog trained to warm the feet of his mistress. Silently, while he slept, she felt over his face lightly with her toe. The second month of their marriage passed this way, with her body inflamed by his nearness. Though his canine countenance expressed no more than a stupid smile, his simple animal nature inspired her, and in dreams she attacked him. *It has grown hot in this lagoon. I shall swim with him. She slipped into the warm water, where his silver face shined. Into his heat she swam.*

She woke, feverish. Her husband's hot breath was on her feet. Unable to resist, she tiptoed on the warm waves from his tongue, dancing there.

*　　*　　*

In the third month, the dog became a tortoise, crawling slowly up the mattress toward her. Each night she felt his shell coming closer. When she looked in the dark purple toward him, he seemed wrinkled as an ancient. His faithful dog-eye was gone and in its place was a wiser, if somewhat frightening beak, and two gleaming eyes, accustomed to the night sea.

She wanted to hide inside the pillow, to shrink into nothingness, to keep herself apart from his breathing on her knees, and from his devious turtle-eyes coldly haunting her.

Daytime brought her release from the illusion. She went to the temple and begged Kali to advise her. The beautiful altar goddess danced on the head of a slave. If only I could be fierce as you, Goddess. The statue was mute. The distraught girl rose and left the temple. Her husband was kneeling in the sand of the temple garden, the sun upon his dark curling hair. If he weren't so shifty, he might almost be good-looking, she thought, walking slowly toward him.

* * *

That night he came slowly toward her, to her thighs with his head. What fiendish ticklement is this, she wondered in a moment of clarity, before the warm cream of his breath poured over her thighs. She pressed them together to stop the sensation and it grew more intense. She spread them apart trying to cool them and her soft leg-flesh touched his nose.

"Yes, Queen," he said in a whisper.

"Please," she said, softly.

"What would you have me do?" asked the turtle.

Could she tell him her thighs were milk? She raised her hips just a little.

"Is there a lump in the mattress, Gracious Saint?"

"Oh, the dog!" she cried and turned quickly away, but her gown rose up so that perhaps he could see the soft underness of her thighs. What an immodesty, she thought, quickly pulling down her gown.

The fourth month of marriage brought the face of her husband directly in line with her secret. His breath upon her toes had been inflaming; his breathing on her rose was driving her insane. Streams of air reached between her thighs, gently handling her flower. She tried always to sleep on her stomach, so she would not be subjected to warm southern winds, but in dreams she soon rolled over again, into the tropic breeze from his nose, which played over the hot little island between her thighs.

Later, when they walked outside, she went head down, deep in confusion. Caught in the rain, she made no attempt to take cover. The cloudburst ran along her hot flesh and her husband stood with her in the rain, and the village women no doubt thought them mad.

*   *   *

At five months, his face lay by her stomach. His breath blew her gown lightly; she touched him with her belly, upon his hooked nose.

His eagle-eye saw through her gown, to the soul in her rolling ocean of jelly, to the eye in her navel. Into that canyon of time went his nose, filling it with warmth. She lay perspiring like a holy woman on a bed of coals, though she did not feel holy, in fact, quite the opposite.

When six months ended, the wandering slave in her bed had lodged at her breasts. His eyes gleamed in the dark like an idol's. The purple light played on his face. She tried to cover her breasts, to hide them from his dark look, but they are so tender, they hurt me, let him look if he dares to. His breath touched her lightly on her soft little island tops, her red-peaked nipples. Excited as if she were dancing in the village, her breasts heaved and touched him. In the crevice of dreams where her heart lay concealed, she enclosed his nose.

It tickled ridiculously. That was its strange power. She was ten-thousand-times-over afraid of it, yet somehow withstood the invasion. Encircle his nose again, my breasts, smother him with your sweetness, drive him mad too.

He remained calm. Yet in the seventh month he was stretched out entirely beside her. Kinglike he slept, lightly, staring sometimes at the ceiling for long hours. Around her body was an envelope of heat, as if she were afloat in a warm cloud. His breath seemed to have lingered all over her body, gathering around it like a mist. His elbow touched her. Quickly she drew her arm away. This bed is far too small for two people. She withdrew to the farthest corner. But in curling up she bumped him with her backside and he, amazingly, returned the bump.

This shocking demonstration was repeated on the following night and on many nights afterward. Like wandering taxis they bumped each other, bumper to bumper they lay pressed together in the street of feathers. It is mad play, but what pleasure. Later she rose up and looked at the impertinent fellow, naked to the waist in the moonlight.

"Yes, Lotus?" He woke and rose to her.

"I'm so thirsty," she said.

"At once," he said, and leapt out of the bed.

He returned with a cool drink of water. She drank it slowly and extended the glass back to him. As he retrieved it, his hand brushed light as a wing-tip across her breast. He put the glass down and crawled into bed beside her. Reaching for the thin sheet, the devil's finger touched her again. Her red breasts heaved to meet his hands, wanting that and wanting more.

On the following night, as he served her milk, she leaned in a most favorable angle and his palm touched underneath her breasts, in the softness, and lingered there.

Next night, she was seated on a cushion by the window. He came from the kitchen on his knees, bearing a tray on which a glass of red wine was balanced. He bowed. His black curling hair was like snakes in a dance. His hand came forward. All night he held the threads of her shoulder straps in his fingertips, and toward dawn he let them drop and half awake, half dreaming, she watched her left moon appear, naked, round, full.

Earlier, in the fashion of the slave girls, she had made herself up, reddening the nipple, tanning the round globe, even underneath, where the sun never came. Now, she dared not move, the silence was all around them. He stared at her breast like a devotee at a statue and she accepted his stare.

For days he stared at it, through the passing light of morning, afternoon, and evening. He pondered it from every angle, looking all around it and underneath it, like a monkey with a problem. She did not know what to do. Her thoughts were jumbled, her head was spinning, for they spent so much time in bed these days. Slowly his hand came forward. Was it an age or an instant that passed, she'd lost touch with time. Suddenly he was touching her on the left breast and fondling it.

So she spent the ninth month, one breast out. Each time she tried to tie her gown up, he untied it again. She felt so odd sitting eating dinner with one breast bare. Shortly after dinner he began stroking the other one, and each night it was the same, until the tenth month came and he slipped the knot on her right shoulder, rendering both breasts bare.

She sat, naked to the waist. All night he sat looking at her, and she at him. She nodded off to sleep finally, and her dreams were filled with insanity. She'd lost sight of father, mother, dignity, the world, except for two moons in the air. She felt a cloudy field all around her and she ran through a ghostly mist, awaking to his lips upon the tiny crater of her right moon.

Then he revolved both moons in his hands, until she was thrashing back and forth on the bed, most indecorously. She begged him to stop revolving them but he laughed and went on revolving them.

That morning she rose early and since she was in the kitchen before him, she prepared her own breakfast, and as an afterthought, prepared his too, and served it to him.

She knelt by the bed and slipped the tray over the covers. He opened his eyes and she lowered her own. He ate quietly and the sunlight came, turning the bed to a gold palanquin on which he seemed to float, looking down on her. She had covered her bosom to serve him. With a gesture of perfect sovereignty, he slipped the knots of her gown and bared her breasts again. He digested his breakfast, fondling them.

About noontime, after five hours of feeling her breasts, he began sucking them, first one, then the other, alternating on the hour. At dinnertime she could not help but scream, so tender had they grown from his feasting. This incredibly idiotic child is draining my soul, sucking it into himself, but she welcomed him nonetheless and in fact offered up to him with her hands the twin fruits.

By night he continued lowering her gown. Inch by inch he pulled it, a little each evening, until her stomach heaved up into the moonlight. Like a vast continent it came into view, but she did not feel continent, in fact, just the opposite, ravished as she was by feverish grindings in her stomach. He squeezed her moons and licked across the land of her belly, his moustache trailing in her navel.

Finally the gown was down to the edge of her secret. In a dream she was taken down the night to an ancient forest altar, a cave in which a priestess dwelled. It was a shimmering red crack in the mountain and she entered. The shining man was sitting on a throne, deep inside the cave.

She woke, moved her legs, felt suddenly free; her gown was gone. He was looking at her dark scented place, which sparkled as if with dewdrops. She felt older, parting her legs, then demurely closed them, feeling childish. He stared at it all night, and continued to stare at it throughout the morning, as the sun rose upon her little tangled grove. He ate lunch looking at it and spent the evening with his nose practically next to it. She felt herself burning alive.

She had to leave the bed. She ran naked through the house. He caught her in the kitchen, in a most peculiar position, putting his hand directly into her forest. She sank to her knees and bowed her head, worshipping him as he ran his finger all along the crack in the forest floor.

For the entire eleventh month he investigated that mysterious forest. He parted the underbrush so that the altar was plainly visible, and then like a blind man feeling letters, he ran his fingers along the sacred tabernacle, reading every wrinkle and fold. The altar streamed with the precious nectar. His finger slipped just the slightest bit inside it and remained there, all day, every day, for a month. She screamed, beating him about the head with her hands.

Silently, day by day, he worked like a hermit drawing with his finger on a cave wall. Then, by night, he brought his head to the cave and spoke a wordless whisper. She pressed her forest lips to his in silent answer and they kissed softly. All night, hour after hour, he kissed her there, while she squirmed, kicking her legs, beating her hands upon the mattress. For a month she writhed, groaning, in and out of delightful anguish.

From the devil he had learned to take in his lips the tiny turned-out root that hung from the mouth of her sacred cave. Known to no one, guarded and carefully hidden by her through all her years, it was now in the man's lips and he was humming on it. The tune was crazy, mad bees swarmed through her, but each time, just as she felt herself about to turn into sweetest honey, he stopped, leaving her hovering, dying, frantic.

They did not go out any longer. When he tried to lift his head away to bring food, she held him by the ears. The food grew cold and she grew hotter, running her fingers through his curly hair.

By day she followed him around the house, served him on her knees, washed his body, made his bed. He had enslaved her with his tongue. Her will was gone, sucked out in the night. Standing by the kitchen doorway, she moved aside to let him pass. His sleeping gown was loose and some devil played it open and she saw the outline of his manhood. He brushed past her and the hot organ touched her thigh.

Later in the day, as she bent over to pick up his slippers, he pressed it against her backside. Day after day then, she encountered it, and in her dreams she saw it standing on the throne inside the altar, shining, one-eyed, on fire.

Unable to resist any longer, she touched it, thinking he was asleep. He was not. He opened his eyes, fully awake.

"Please," she said. It was the twelfth month and she stretched out on the bed and spread her legs like a courtesan. Her forest stream was flowing, she was made of liquid, her body was undone, the veils of her passion unknotted.

"Please," she said, taking his member in her hand. He rose and knelt between her legs. Then he braced himself over her and slowly, like a man falling in a dream, lowered himself.

The night fell upon her. His thighs rested on hers and against her altar she felt the hot hard pressing, not of a fist or a finger, but of a finer thing, a more distinguished tool, of shape divine, like the shining thing in her dreams, and she longed to take it into herself. She pressed her forest crack against the fleshy head, feeling its wet eyedrop. She nibbled with her clumsy forest lips, dumbly trying to swallow the burning Godhead.

Each night for a week it played at her melting doorway, and just when she thought she could stand its presence, it entered the buttery folds and she gasped with amazement for she could not stand it, so painful and terrible was it, at last. She gave her hips just the slightest move, to appreciate her agony better.

"Don't move," he said in a dark voice beside her ear, and she didn't.

They lay that way each night for a week, like trees fallen together in a storm. Her legs entangled his, locking at the ankles, and her tiny cave-root was engaged.

Pressing deeper each night, he soon reached the tiny red curtain across her virgin altar. He pressed harder, but the way was small, the pressure unbearable. The space is too tight, she thought, weeping. I can never fit this thing into me, it is unendurable, it . . . seems to be going in a little farther.

No longer a virgin, she howled, for the jewel of the moon was red with blood. The veil is burning, the veil is gone. God's body slipped slowly into her.

Wheels of flame revolved in her brain and in the forest

cave the Godhead reigned, solemn, still, supreme, and she felt the beat of his burning heart-shape.

All night they lay that way, he did not allow her to move, but surreptitiously she managed to, flexing the tiny muscles of her secret mouth. Each time she did lights appeared to her and her warm tears flowed. The dreams of mating danced round her, encircling her, and she was their center and her hair was entwined with his. There was a beat, it is slow, this coming of beauty, and their locked bodies brought it nearer, so that by dawn it had almost arrived.

The need for nourishment finally overtook them and that afternoon he withdrew the Godhead from her and her cave closed shut. This is reality, she thought, stumbling naked toward the kitchen. She fried them lunch, a festival of grains, and naked they ate, lightly.

At sundown she lay down again and parted her legs. We are on the mountain of pleasure. It goes into me again. I am reassured of its constancy. I am . . . quite full, dearest, come closer.

When it was fully lodged in her, she spread her legs into a wide V, and raising them into the air, kicked them about, laughing madly, with elephants dancing, serpents too, and she walked in her brain, room by room, through waking dreams, down the road of joy, tossing, turning, coming closer, to the mysterious presence. Panting, sweating, she held his buttocks, tried to make him move, to take them closer.

Not until the thirteenth month did he move, but that movement was definitive, marking a farther outpost of bliss. To feel his tool run in and out of me, that is the deep truth. Could there be more? She suspected another door.

Each night he stroked her once, so slowly, the entire night was needed for the length of his thousand-armed shaft to move in and out. At times she thought it was not moving at all, but it was, and in the extremities of slowness she saw concealed worlds.

Time changed; in a single second she saw great lengths of his organ. Breathless, afire, stupefied, she too learned to move slowly. Here the moment opens. In it are contained like tiny seeds a million more divisions. And she grew smaller.

It was the end of the thirteenth month. She loved him but wanted to reach their plateau, the resting spot. I am so hot. He is boiling me. Still they went more slowly. She fell through enormous canyons of time, down the deep pocket of pleasure, swooning ever more slowly into the depths of delight. She heard dragons roaring, such a slow grinding noise, such a slow turning.

They ate only liquids, some ethereal force seeming to sustain them now, for they lost no weight, but grew light as lamps. His countenance became magical. In his face she saw blue God-masks, jewels, crowns. The sound, the sound of their divine grinding surrounded them. No longer human, they lived outside of time.

The beautiful presence came, as he touched her in the womb, and like spring burst forth. I am creation. From her came the universe, that was the roar. From her came worlds, she was their door. Spread across the galaxies, she moved her body slowly, coming everywhere, at once, very wise.

In the beat of moons, not seconds, he stroked her, so say the Scriptures.

Postcard Found
in a Trunk

"Tha's the jail," said the cab driver as we entered San Francisco. "You don' wanta spend any time there."

The cab moved on through the Tenderloin section, where something other than tenderness, but certainly involving loins, was for sale. The driver took us to the wrong hotel, then backed up around the corner and dropped us off. I collapsed in our room, but my companion, the lovely Monica, wanted to go out, at once.

Somnambulistically, I followed her, back to the elevator and out into Chinatown. It was the New Year and I stepped on a firecracker, which blew a hole in the sole of my shoe, stimulating acupressure points 5 through 42.

"You can buy a pair of Tai Chi slippers," said Monica.

We started up one of those ominous hills, famous in

story and song for giving you knotted balls in your calf. In Tai Chi slippers it was all the worse, but we reached the top and there was the town below, struck by the late afternoon sun, firecrackers resounding in its canyons.

Had Lao Tzu felt this way as he went through the Pass at Chou?

The hilltop had many gardens, exotic foliage neatly trimmed. Turning, I saw a street sign marked Vallejo. "I know a guy who lives on this street," I said, and we followed numbers, as the sun went down. We were now able to look into windows, observing the intimate lifestyle of San Franciscans.

"Look at that chandelier," said Monica.

And paper lanterns, half-hidden behind ornate screens. We got to my friend's house, but he'd moved.

Then it was dark and Tiffany lamps provided the warm colors of astral worlds, with an antique motorcycle in a saloon window, shining. There were elegant figures in the lamplight, glasses in hand, smiling, chatting about life in the local dream. We had dropped from the sky, Monica and I, and caused the angles of the night to change, just slightly; the saloon shifted, disturbed by our gaze, and rotated out of sight. After all, there were already too many tourists in this town.

"Lemme look in a phone book, I'll find his new address."

Monica had a map torn from the hotel magazine, the streets drawn comically, the kind of map that destroys equilibrium, and we followed it.

We found my friend's house and rang the buzzer.

Turning the first landing, I saw his door open. He didn't recognize me until I called his name. It had been fifteen years.

"Come on in," he said. He was the editor of a literary magazine. "I can't work for anybody anymore," he said.

"I know how you feel."

"So I started the magazine and I'm living on food stamps."

I'd been dreaming about him, off and on, for fifteen years, as someone I'd probably never see again, and here we were visiting; he said he had to go to the movies. Could we meet him at the magazine offices in the morning?

Monica and I, back in the dark street: "He looks good."

"His hair has gone gray."

We climbed the high hills, and now the lights of the city were twinkling below.

*   *   *

"Come on in," he said in the morning. "Take a chair."

"This office is alright."

"The rent's high, but I try not to pay it."

"I saw a nice café on the corner."

"The landlord owns it, we can't go there."

The shelves were filled with heavy volumes; the walls carried posters of bygone literary periods. "I'm borrowed up to the eyeballs," he said.

Beside a picture of Joyce was an enlarged photostat of a government check for $12,000 given to the magazine.

He saw my gaze and said, "I spent it in an afternoon."

In the other room were three young people, working for the magazine, for nothing, he said, to gain experience in publishing. "Of course, since there are no publishing houses out here, it won't do them any good."

We departed, going back into the bright day. He led us up a little alleyway. "That's where Lennie Bruce fell out of the window and broke both legs."

I felt the comedian's vertigo, and other pieces of legend, floating in the sunshine. The ferns in a doorway had long memories, and what of the bricks? Monica said something about shanghaied sailors. The white walls radiated more than sunlight back at us.

"That's my landlord's place, we cross here."

We passed the Café Trieste, where Jack Kerouac had hung out, in a time that had once been the only time there was; if you like Chinese puzzles, the twisted nail, contemplate that elusive moment in which travelers celebrated the new era in American letters.

I took a footstep and felt it sinking, endlessly, in San Francisco.

"The values out here—" said our friend. "Some people I know gave their child a pet chicken to teach him responsibility."

"That is odd."

"I tried to borrow money from them."

We walked to the top of a great hill. "And there's Columbus." He pointed to a statue overlooking the bay. In one hand of the statue was a chiseled piece of paper, which, our guide said, contained an order for one pizza to go, with anchovies. I gazed with Columbus across the water.

A mild breeze moved on the heights, Monica's hair blown by it, and I tried to live in the moment, though there is always the tendency to say to oneself that the experience will only become meaningful later on, in retrospect.

"There was an interesting robbery recently," said our friend. "A Latino stuck up a grocery store with a banana."

We descended, into Chinatown again, and I bought a size 57 worker's cap from Peking.

"I'd like to go to Williams-Sonoma," said Monica.

"What's that?" asked our friend.

"A gourmet cookery shop."

He shook our hands goodbye, and we watched him walk off, into the memory from which he'd come; I knew that we were being filed in the same way in his mind, beside debts, book reviews, and a man armed with a banana. He grew smaller, turned a corner, vanished without a ripple. Do either of us exist, I wondered? If Kerouac and Bruce are gone, along with ancient Chinese emperors? Only the city lives on, a shocking thought, each of us particles of its dream, bright particles, fading particles, dead suns of San Francisco.

We were heading toward Williams-Sonoma, entering into a cheerful banquet, with pretty tablecloths and a wicker picnic basket for the boot of your Bentley. I sat down, exhausted, while Monica shopped. My size 57 hat from Peking was giving me a headache. I closed my eyes, and historic meals of the city came before my eyes, attended by women in velvet gowns and men in silk hats; they were whirled away on a great gleaming disc, and became dolls in miniature, moving stiffly, then ceasing to move, then gone.

"You're angry at me for taking so long," said Monica.

"Hell, no," I said, getting up. We had supper and night fell and then we were whirling on the disc, little old figures imagined by some future traveler with a backward glance. I woke the next morning, with Monica opening the distortion map on the bed. "The cable car will take us all the way to the waterfront."

We rode the bizarre vehicle in the postcard, and suddenly we were staring across the water at Alcatraz. The tour boat was loading to go; for a couple of dollars you can visit. I put a quarter in a telescope, as close as I cared to get, but it wouldn't focus.

"On this very spot . . ." said a taped voice.

The ghosts of old criminals could not help shaking their heads at people paying for the ride.

"I'm going to visit the Chocolate Factory," said Monica.

"I'll be on the pier." I boarded a Scottish merchant, built in 1886. The smells in the gallery remained, of biscuits and pies and various stews absorbed into the woodwork. A skeleton crew remains too, you can see them gliding silently past the lanterns.

Monica found me in the hold, staring at a shaft of sunlight, down which numerous spirits could easily come, up which others could go.

"Look in there," I said, pointing to a shadowy chamber, where a seaman with a lamp once guided the anchor chain into place.

The world is filled with ghosts, tour guides for the traveler. Inside the chain locker is a ladder, aslant in the streaming light, the wood dark, suggestive . . .

Monica dragged us on to other things; but you have already gotten the point, if there is one—what you see isn't so important, and you must not ignore the dead. We rode the number 30 bus, and the 28, a long ways, all around the edges of the city. I saved the wrinkled transfer, for like every thoughtful dog I know there is a secret path through these parks and pavilions. Ask the driver for any stop at all, the ghostly guides are with you; the wheels of the bus are the wheels of chance.

Spinning, spinning . . .

In that saloon, beneath those bright lamps, a gentleman raises his glass.

A young woman climbs a flight of stairs toward a Victorian house.

Any of these sights will be the center of the world.

The stones have remarked you. The ferns have remembered. A comedian is falling backward from his window.

Sun, Moon, and Storm

"Antonio, please open the shutters," said the whore.

Antonio Allegri da Correggio sat on the edge of the bed, staring at the floor. His body ached from fever, and he had no strength. He had slept again in his clothes, too weary to remove them. It had come again to gnaw at him, the rat of Mantua.

The whore rose up on one elbow and stroked the back of his neck. "Are you feeling alright?"

He walked to the window and opened the shutters. The light was pale rose cast on high clouds. In the distance was the Cathedral of Parma, and within its high graceful tower was the vision, waiting to devour what was left of him.

The prostitute bathed and then slowly toweled herself

dry, for she knew he liked to study her that way, with the towel draped around her. The room was hers, the walls covered with sketches he'd made of her, the woman in them a creature created by a man's hand, and it troubled her, and pleased her, and finally left her with an inexplicable feeling concerning this Antonio Allegri. It was not a simple situation, having one's soul mirrored like that, the part a prostitute never gives. But in the end, she supposed, to someone somewhere, one finally surrenders all, and he was at least a gentleman. "I'm in love with you," she said, making a joke of it, and throwing the towel at him.

"That's because I stay with you and can't pay you anything." He too tried to joke, but the five hundred gold ducats he'd received from the Canon were gone now and so were the last three years he'd spent working on the Canon's cathedral, and it was no joke. "I must finish it," he said, staring out the window at the dome of the cathedral, while she dressed. "Once, you know, when I first discovered my talent, I thought I would be rich."

"Once," said the whore, putting on her cloak and joining him at the door, "before I discovered my talent, I thought I would live in a villa with a husband and children and flowers."

They descended to the street, where the heat of summer radiated off the hard-packed earth. His footsteps were slow, and his tall body bent at the shoulders, huddled inside ragged clothes.

"It was in Mantua," he said. They turned into a shady courtyard, where massive vines were entwined around an old tree. A group of young people had gathered there, singing to the viol and guitars. "I was ruined by the plague." He stopped, to listen to the music.

She put her arm through his, and felt his dizzy swaying. He was a young man already old, his hair and beard turned gray, his face graying too, like ashes in a dead fire. "Let us eat," she said, nodding toward the cavern in the courtyard.

"Later," he said. "You can bring me something later." He walked on through the courtyard, toward the cathedral.

The heavy wooden door strained him, and he cursed the plague and Mantua and himself. They entered the familiar gloom in which souls prayed. A long aisle led to where he himself prayed, on a scaffold fifty feet above the altar. It repelled him, its platforms and ladders suggesting only difficult labor. He wanted to eat though he had no appetite, for if he ate a great deal he'd grow tired and his ambition would be drained. I'll sit on this floor, with a large meal inside me, and I won't be able to move. I'll sleep then, quietly.

His footsteps carried him up the aisle toward the scaffolding, and he felt the impossibility of exerting himself further. Through the network of planks and ladders, he saw his beautiful beings ascending the sides of the dome. The Virgin soared off into the very center, where a brilliant sun was receiving her. Its light streamed through the Virgin and illuminated a ring of angels rejoicing in space. Below them, on the lower slopes of the wall were the saints, on whom the light fell more gently, diffused by its long journey.

He gripped the ladder, and began the climb. The odor

of his paints grew stronger, held in the cup of the dome, and what strength he found seemed to come from them and the memories they stirred in his blood. With them he closed his fingers, and by them he pulled higher, into the loftier regions of his dome, among his saints and angels. Their faces and attitudes had revealed themselves to him slowly, and now he knew them intimately, these hidden aspects of himself—creatures of fever, dream, and vision, faces of the living and the dead, and the never-to-be.

Slowly, in the very middle of the bowl of glorious color, he mixed his tints. The painted flesh radiated power; he felt his angels looming over him with their mysterious gestures, whose meaning he would never understand.

"A shadow here—" he said to an angel hanging just beyond the edge of the highest plank. "It sets you free from your clouds, lightens your lovely goose feather wings . . ."

He muttered to his creations, as he walked back and forth among them on his scaffold. They were mostly finished, and a sane man would have called it complete and gone home to bed.

"He isn't feeling well and he will not eat," said the prostitute to Padre Dominic, a young priest of the cathedral, and the model for Saint John—a youthful and delicate John, his eyes a mixture of puzzlement and awe at a great mystery, which was indeed how Padre Dominic perceived the beautiful dome in which he himself was depicted ten times larger than life.

"Come down, Antonio, you cannot work without eating!" The prostitute had gotten soup and bread for the painter, and for herself. She was required to stay the long day with him, for she was the model for the Virgin. "You know," she said, turning back to Padre Dominic now, "until I took him home with me, he was sleeping on the stone floor there—" She pointed with her spoon. "—beneath his precious ceiling."

"I wouldn't worry about him," said Padre Dominic. "The way he has made all this appear shows great reserves of strength." The young priest gestured toward the ceiling—to the living circle of flesh, arms and legs entwined, bare limbs of every size and shape in every possible position.

"And what does the Canon say?" asked the prostitute.

Padre Dominic cast a nervous glance toward the side door of the cathedral. "He doesn't say a word."

"He is to pay Antonio another hundred gold ducats."

"Oh, I'm certain—" The young priest gestured again toward the ceiling. "Such beautiful work—"

"Beauty is often cheated." The prostitute turned back to the soup, stirring its steaming contents.

"I'll carry it up to him," said the priest, and began the ascent of the scaffold, toward the tiny, shabby, human figure in among the gigantic angels. Padre Dominic, though young, had heard the souls of men in confession, but he did not claim to know the soul of this man, more solitary than a monk in his attitudes and, at times, demonic in his ambition. "I've brought you food," said Padre Dominic, offering the bowl.

The painter took the bowl and drained it quickly. The

rich spicy liquid on his tongue dazzled him for a moment, and he felt the twinge of old longing, to lie down, to curl asleep in a mother's arms, but he kept his eyes fixed on the ceiling.

"Would you and our friend Mary please take your positions? Just for a short while . . ."

The priest called to the prostitute and she climbed slowly up through the scaffolding, until she and the priest were on the heights of the staging, in the position to which the painter had trained them. Padre Dominic disrobed and raised his arms in saintly gesture.

"The Canon is an honest man?" asked Mary, settling herself, so that her legs beneath her robe shaped the material into the outline of a great heart.

"Without question, honest," said Padre Dominic, trying to produce an air of confidence. But his tone lacked conviction; the Canon was known to be eccentric at times.

"You look troubled, Padre," said Mary, gazing at the priest, his young figure framed in the candlelight.

He glanced at her, then looked away, back toward the dome. "In the presence of all this—" He nodded toward the soaring figures, so vital and so gracefully formed. "—I realize I have no gift."

"Every man has a certain gift," said the mother of God. "But sometimes he needs a woman to bring it out."

"I'm a renunciate!" said the priest, looking quickly away, but not that quickly, reflected the prostitute. "It's all so strange," she said with a sigh.

"Strange? What is strange?" asked Correggio from his ladder, then turned away from any answer. Of course it is strange, foreshortening of this degree. He descended the ladder, paced along the planks, and felt that his teacher would have approved. As always, when thinking of Mantegna, he thought of Rome, which he had yet to visit, where the greatest marvels of all were housed, and where his study would be completed. But a wave of dizziness interrupted his thought, and he was forced to grip the scaffold tightly. It will not do to have the artist plunge into his paintpots, not just yet.

If I can get to Rome, he thought, laying his head against a strong crossbeam and closing his eyes till the dizziness passed. There the last refinement will come. I'm only forty. There's still time.

*   *   *

They walked through the evening shadows of the street. The lamps were being lit and the window of the apothecary shop held the last streak of light the day had to offer. The prostitute followed him into the shop and sniffed among the bowls of dried herbs.

"Can you make up my tea," said the painter. "I'll paint you another small canvas of your children."

"You're not looking well, Signore," said the druggist, mixing up the potion.

"The rat of Mantua is nibbling at me," said the painter. "But we have an agreement, the rat and I."

*   *   *

In the night Antonio Allegri held her, fascinated by each golden thread of her hair, threads which he'd labored to match, drawing them out in fine strands. Perhaps they do it better in Rome, or perhaps not. It's as fine as I can do, that's certain.

"*Antonio,*" she whispered, rubbing her face on his broad chest. His pain was hidden, the way he hid anger, jealousy, most things, driving it all into his will and fingertips, but she knew his suffering anyway, had come to read it from his eyelids, his breath, his silences. He was a man who'd studied, whose thoughts were colors, but she understood him because he was lost, here in Parma, because he was alone and desperate. He didn't need her, he'd sleep on stone, and for that reason she'd opened her sanctuary to him. He'd covered it with drawings of her, and the moonlight touched them now, transforming her yet again, into something that only the moon and an artist's hand could make of her.

*   *   *

At midnight, they rose for his medicine. He swallowed it, then took his sketchbook and began drawing a young woman, small and thin, with delicate features. Her face and figure were rendered quickly, as if it were an exercise he'd often performed.

"Who is she?" asked the prostitute.

"My wife."

"She's very beautiful."

"She died in Mantua." He turned the page, started another. "Here are the two children." With equal swiftness, he pictured a small boy and girl.

"Where are they now?"

"In my village, in Correggio. I must go back there soon."

56

"Send for your children. I'll care for them here."

"They're with their grandmother. It's better there."

She refilled his cup with the herbal concoction. He drank it slowly, knowing it was hopeless. But perhaps, he reflected, there will be a doctor in Rome.

*   *   *

They sat together in the front row of the cathedral, on a paint-spattered cloth. Antonio Allegri's head was back and he was gazing at his dome. She worked, sewing a patch on his ragged coat. "You look like a beggar."

He didn't answer her, his attention far off, on the giant curving bowl above him. "I see where I could put in another corps of cherubs, and opposing them a row of green-gold demons."

"Finish it, for the love of God." She flopped his coat over, to a nearly severed sleeve.

He closed his eyes. "A duck, a horse, a thousand riders. Whatever I wish to see, I see in perfect detail. Is this a blessing?"

"I close my eyes and see us," she said, "far from here, in circumstances that can never be. So what use is it? It serves only to torment."

He heaved himself up with a sigh, went to his ladder and began his climb. Padre Dominic entered quietly through the side door. "Good day, Padre," said Antonio Allegri, as he climbed upward.

"Good day, Maestro," said the priest, and crossed in front of the altar, where he knelt, and then turned to where the prostitute was sitting. "Good day," he said, coming to the pew beside her. "How is he today?" he asked.

"Suffering, of course," she said. "Tortured by his vision."

"I have no vision," said the young priest. "I haven't suffered enough, I suppose."

"Do you want to?" asked the prostitute, her eyes soft upon him.

*　　*　　*

Night was on the cathedral. Gazing through the narrow windows of the dome, Antonio Allegri stared across the darkened city, to the city walls. Beyond them a column of smoke was rising from the camp of the barbarians who had begun their threat upon the town. He studied the smoke and compared it with the painted clouds which played among his saints and angels. He worked through the night, laying new and more delicate veils of vapor on the ceiling. At dawn the campfires disappeared, and it was learned that the barbarians had moved on, deciding against invasion. Antonio Allegri sent word to the Canon that the dome of the cathedral was done and would the Canon be so kind as to authorize payment as agreed upon.

*　　*　　*

"A stew of frogs," said the Canon, staring at the ceiling.

Antonio Allegri lowered his head and looked at the floor. He did not want to look up and see his painting. He knew how suggestible he was, knew that he might look up and see exactly what the Canon was seeing, a mad jumble of legs, sticking out every which way from a smoking stewpot.

"... *stew of frogs ... of frogs ...*" The Canon's voice echoed in the great dome, reverberating among the angels.

"Even so, Excellency, it's three years' labor and the stew must be paid for."

"Impossible. You've desecrated the House of God."

"An illusion."

"Signor Allegri, I'm afraid—"

"Not nearly so afraid as you will be, Excellency, after I hire an old woman of Correggio to perform a certain ceremony in your name—" Antonio Allegri watched the blood leave the Canon's face. "Some say she is a ridiculous old woman," smiled the painter. "Others, who have lost certain valuable possessions, such as their noses, think differently."

* * *

When he went to collect the money, he found that instead of gold, he had been paid in coppers, which were in a large sack. Padre Dominic stood beside it in the doorway of the cathedral, his face covered in sadness and shame. "I'll call for a carriage," said the young priest.

"And who'll pay for it, Padre?" asked the painter, giving the great sack a kick with his toe, measuring its weight.

The young priest looked down at the floor. Antonio

Allegri smiled at him and said, "You and I have taken the vow of poverty, Padre, because wealth is such a burden." He bent over and gripped the sack in both hands, hoisting it upward. "You see me, while I'm wealthy, struggling with riches." Padre Dominic helped him settle the sack onto his shoulders, and the painter swayed for a moment under the weight, but bending forward a bit he gained his balance.

"I must go now, Padre. I have a distance to travel. Please tell our friend Mary that the Canon settled his debt. She was concerned for the condition of his soul."

Padre Dominic brightened. "Our friend Mary is going to take the veil."

"She's lying," said Antonio Allegri. "She'll take your veil first." He walked forward into the road, leaving the priest, the cathedral, the ceiling.

After passing through the gates of the city, he was alone on the road. The sky was clear, the sun bright. The fields rolled on and away. So the Canon has had his little joke. Coppers! If only I knew an old woman.

The day was hot and walking difficult. But I know how to balance a load. If shouldered correctly, a great amount of weight can be managed.

The road went uphill and down. Antonio Allegri walked the miles slowly, and then more slowly. The sack is a tremendous thing, like a domed ceiling. When you first grab for it, it seems like an easy job, but it gets heavier. As time goes on it gets heavier.

He felt the fever stirring in him again, accompanied by a dull ache in his bones. Someday, when I pass this way again, I shall paint that field there, for the effect of the sun on the grain.

The sweat ran into his eyes and onto his lips. The fever grew brighter, until his ears were roaring with the flame of it. In Mantua, there was such a fire, when they collected the bodies and burned them. It's just my blood, pounding.

The Canon thinks I'll lay my load down, and that he will come and claim it. But I don't bend so easily.

He watched his feet as they moved below in the dust, within his comfortable old shoes. Then suddenly he was staring directly at the dust, the tiny grains of earth only inches from his eyes. The sack of coppers was across his back, pinning him to the ground. He tried to move, but the sack held him. Surely I can move it . . . surely . . .

His exertions fanned the fever in his brain; his head felt crowned with thorns and the sweat dripping past his eyes to the ground seemed like glittering beads of blood. He closed his eyes and the forms in his head swirled up, combining and recombining—bathers, Christs, and goddesses, sun, moon, and storm, the faces rich and perfect, without a brushstroke discernible. They melted and mixed, becoming a single masterful design.

He struggled to rise, as the world of the mind shone before him. If only I hadn't attempted to place the cathedral on my back. I've stumbled with it and it's crushed me.

He tried to open his eyes but the sunlight hurt him and he closed them again, seeing with great satisfaction *The Fates*—favorite of all the paintings he'd done. The three beautiful women of the painting smiled at him, but went about their work, the lovely Clotho holding the staff on which the thread of life was wound, her fair sister, Lachesis, drawing forth its determined length. The third sister, Atropos, holding the scissors of fate in her hand, became the rat of Mantua, who nibbled through the silver thread, severing it.

*   *   *

With great embarrassment, Padre Dominic presented himself to the heirs of Antonio Allegri, deceased painter of Correggio. Flushed and hesitant, he delivered the demand made by the Canon of the Cathedral of Parma, that the final payment made to the painter, equal to one hundred gold ducats, be returned.

The Canon, it was pointed out, held an agreement signed by Antonio Allegri, which was the lawful contract for the painting of the dome, as well as the arcade, the pillars, the niches, and all the wall space down to the floor. Only the dome had been finished and it, the Canon declared, was an outrage.

With great reluctance and still greater fear of the high offices of the Church, the grandmother of the two Allegri children gave up the sack of coppers.

Several years later, the Canon conceived a plan to efface the painting that had so desecrated the place of worship. Charles V, visiting the cathedral at the time, had to step around buckets of white-wash with which the good friars of the church were preparing to cover the dome. Accompanying him was the great master, Titian. The two travelers and their host, the Canon, stood beneath the dome. Titian, after staring in silence for some time at the rim of human and divine figures ascending there, said quietly, "Turn it upside down, and fill it with gold; even so, you will not have paid its true price."

In this way, the painting was saved, but centuries of perfumed smoke from the frankincense burning daily on the altar below slowly covered the assumption of Mary among the saints and angels with a thick film of grease, leaving visible here and there only a hand, a foot, rising out of what seemed to be a dark smoking stewpot.

Tell Her You Love Her
with a Ring from
DAVE'S HOUSE OF
DIAMONDS

Music Lake was at the top of Music Mountain, a few miles out of town. It was exclusive in that Jews and speedboats were not allowed on the lake, but it was not a rich man's retreat. The fishing was poor and the water cold; the cottages that ringed it were modest summer dwellings belonging to a coal dealer, a furniture salesman, an undertaker, and other middle-class vacationers.

The lifeguard was Gary Gerrity—a powerful swimmer and good-natured bully who kept the children in fear of him. He was proud of his lifeguard's jacket and the whistle which he blew throughout the day. His presence at the beach lent the necessary shadow to keep it from being a riot of fun and splashing, for when he was around the air was filled with words of drowning and rescue. To impress mothers with the dignity of his office, in red and white trunks and jacket, whistle screeching, he often dangled in front of them the image of a bloated corpse he'd seen pulled out of an unguarded lake.

That summer he was involved with Stella Lavelle, a tall beautiful creature, shy, pale, abstracted. She walked with him at night, and went for rides in his car, and parked with him on dark roads, but seemed faraway, as if remembering, or dreaming, of someone else.

Gerrity made a great show of their romance, pressing her close on the square-dance floor every Saturday night, keeping the other young men at a distance from her with threatening glances. The only one who challenged Gerrity's exclusive hold on Stella was the square-dance fiddler, a bony, spectral gambler in iridescent cowboy shirt who flirted openly with Stella, and danced with her, wildly stamping his feet and making the old pavilion echo with his whoops and shouts, which all the Music Lakers loved. Gerrity looked on, smiling at the summer fun, and secretly wanting to murder the fiddler in the moonlight. But there was something in those hollow hillbilly eyes that paralyzed Gerrity's courage, and he was still more weakened by the look which Stella always wore when she returned from the fiddler's dancing, something sad in her eyes, whose mystery made her all the more beautiful to Gerrity, flaming the tormented ecstasy of his love.

He increased his attention, growing tyrannical with her. She grew irritable, and several times broke away from him on the dance floor. Even the children were aware of the uneasy state of the affair: when Gerrity came to the beach in his red jacket the little girls whispered and giggled, and the little boys disobeyed his orders.

Gerrity purchased an engagement ring in town. The ring represented the whole of his summer wages, but as he drove back up to the top of Music Mountain with the precious gem in his pocket, he felt he had crushed the opposition. It was now late August. Soon they would be leaving the lake and returning to school, and Stella would be surrounded by other chances. But she would have his ring, the little glittering chip of his heart, and she would be caught in the diamond's blue-white spell. At evening, as they sat alone on the dock, Gerrity gave Stella the ring and she flung it in the lake.

Next day no swimmers were allowed in the water. Gerrity was diving with a snorkel mask. The beach was crowded with children, teenagers, adults, who cheered him on as he went down. Again and again he dove through the cold green water to the puzzling bottom. All was quiet there, except for the bubbling of his mask, as he picked his way through the tangled weeds, and slowly lifted each stone.

Disturbance Reported on a Pipeline

"There are local superstitions about this rock," said the driver, pointing to the towering pillar that rose into the desert sky.

"Is that so?" said Burgoine, not interested. They had come across the border from Israel and were in the Euphrates valley, near Al Kufah. Their packs were filled with explosives, and Burgoine did not give a damn about the huge rock beneath which they were camped.

"I regret I cannot relate the superstitions to you," said the driver, "but I am faulty in the dialect."

"It doesn't matter," said Burgoine.

"It might have passed the time," said the driver.

Their camp was hidden and protected by rocks. Should a patrol come upon them, their papers identified them as a French archeological expedition, under the favor of the Iraqi Department of Antiquities. This cover was worthless, for if they were handed over to the Directorate of Security, the papers would bounce and they would enjoy imprisonment in Bagdad. Their interrogation, performed by a specialist from Turkey, would be delightful. Burgoine broke open the submachine gun and cleaned the already glistening barrel.

The driver, like most Bedouins, enjoyed talk, especially at night by the fire. "The holy men of our tribe once said I had *wajh khayr*—a lucky face."

"Go to sleep in your lucky face," said Burgoine. "I'll keep watch."

Seeing that his employer was not a man who appreciated the beauty of campfire conversation, the driver crawled into his bag and was instantly asleep. Burgoine watched the driver's chest rise and fall, regularly. The driver knew the desert, and knew how to keep a jeep running. They would reach the oil line tomorrow evening, at Ar Rutbah. They would explode the line northeast of the pumping station, then drive to the main highway, and be swallowed there in the traffic to Bagdad.

Burgoine watched the red light of a plane winking across the stars and wished himself on it, seated in amongst the sleeping passengers. Then the droning of the plane was gone and he gave the driver's bag a kick. "Tell me about the petroleum police."

"The petroleum police," said the driver, instantly awake to the conversation, "are of the least noble blood."

"What about communications and transport?"

"A thing to be despised."

"You're certain of this?"

"We will die of old age before they catch us."

Burgoine withdrew the archeologist's map from his jacket. The driver's snoring resumed, and Burgoine studied the map, trying to make sense out of it. The cities upon it were the buried cities of ancient history, and its roads traced the routes of Xenophon, Alexander, and Julian in their war marches. Burgoine drew some lines lightly on the map, then erased them. The flames of the campfire rose up in a final brilliant burst and receded into embers, and he could no longer see clearly.

He watched out over the stone wastes. Nothing could approach them from behind, for it was rock wall. And then to disprove this, he heard a footstep behind him, and his mind was suddenly racing, making curious connections—a certain café appearing and a woman's face passing on the Rue des Malmaisons on a night of no particular significance, and this went on alone and apart from the physical reality of the cloaked figure he saw slip out from behind the rock.

Burgoine's submachine gun came up; the cloaked figure spun toward him, raising a hand, drawing it back, sending a knife through the starlight.

Burgoine ducked it, but something stayed his finger on the trigger of his own weapon, because of the incredible nature of the movements now being made by the cloaked man, who had thrown no knife, who was only thrusting both hands forward, again and again, making hypnotic gestures at Burgoine.

Burgoine walked toward the little man, who continued

his gesturing, splaying his fingers out in tense design, then coiling them back and shooting them out again.

"Here now," said Burgoine, grabbing hold of the man's wrist.

The man started babbling, and made various signs in the air, as if talking the language of the deaf.

"What have we caught?" asked the driver, taking hold of the little man's other arm and questioning him in the language of the desert. The little man answered, with Burgoine scrutinizing him carefully. His cloak hung in many threadbare patches. The eyes were not afraid, but seemed slightly mad or deeply outraged.

"He says he came to pray," said the driver.

"Tell him he's a thief."

The driver translated; the little man replied with a hissing invective, and made several more finger gestures at Burgoine, then pointed at the rock.

"He says he is a priest of Marduk. This is Marduk's rock."

"Bring him over to the fire."

"I thought perhaps we might torture him," said the driver, stirring up the embers.

"No, tell him to sit down. We've got to hang onto him until dawn. Then we'll go our way and he can go his."

"If you are not going to torture him, permit me to return to my sleep. I was dreaming of the Sabaean women, than which there are none more beautiful."

"Find out who Marduk is," said Burgoine. "Headquarters should know if a new chief has taken control of this area."

"I may have to use force."

"You're big on torture, aren't you."

"I was once a candidate for the police force," said the nomad proudly, and menaced the little man with a piece of burning wood, but the captive was not reluctant to talk, and the driver translated.

"I am the son of the son of the golden chain of sons of the priests of Marduk. All the ancient spells are mine, but they no longer work." He made a hypnotic gesture toward Burgoine again.

"He says that a magic knife should have pierced your heart."

"Tell him he should be better armed."

"Alas, the faith has been destroyed," said the priest, through the hesitant translation of the driver. "That is why my magic no longer works. It does not even work on lizards any longer, though last year it worked on a toad." The priest gestured toward the great open waste that surrounded the rock pillar, his ragged sleeves billowing against the stars.

"This plain was once filled with the hundred thousand faithful who worshipped the One God, the Mighty, the Omnipotent, the All-wise Marduk." He raised his arms again and spread them wide, as if raining down a blessing on the hundred thousand worshippers of old.

"Ask him if Marduk is still around," said Burgoine, trying to keep it all in perspective for headquarters.

"Flower-maids came in carloads," said the distraught priest, ignoring the question. "They circled the great tower of the illustrious God, strewing flowers, and then laid themselves down before the priests at the base of the tower. Marduk loves women and in the great days cast Himself into a thousand priests at once, that His enjoyment might be enormous and befitting His divine taste. Alas, there are no more flower-maids." The priest sighed and beat his breast with a slow tattoo of his fists.

"I understand how he feels," said Burgoine. "No more flower-maids. Ask him again where Marduk is camped."

The priest lowered his knees to the sand and bowed his head to the great stone behind them, his voice going low. "Marduk abides in His Heaven, where He has always been. Alas, His Heaven too is empty. Once it held the hundred thousand faithful, and once this pillar of rock was covered with the magic constitution of his reign."

The priest lifted his head and pointed to various parts of the rock, but Burgoine saw only beaten stone, cracked by time and smoothed by rain. "Must have been a long time ago."

"It was in the time of Hammurabi," said the priest. "Then Marduk was mighty in battle, leading the people to triumph and establishing the borders of His kingdom."

"Hammurabi?" Burgoine looked at the driver.

"Yes, he says that all this happened in Bab-elim, in Babylon, two thousand years ago. I am glad now we did not torture him. It is not good to torture the insane."

"Ask him if he's seen any patrols lately."

The driver asked, but the priest seemed not to be listening. His eyes had welled with tears, and his cheeks became bright with them, as he spoke softly into the fire. "The cloak I wear—" He pointed to different parts of the faded patchwork. "—contains pieces of the ancient vestments. I am the only priest of Marduk left, and I carry the ear-whispered secrets of the God in my heart, secrets whispered from one priest to another, down through the Ten Times." The priest's voice went low, as he rocked in the firelight. "I am the only worshipper left. The God's reign has ended. I know that He must die. His once-beautiful clothes are in disarray, just as is the face of His tower."

"Does he see this God?"

"I see Him in my mist."

"That is the word he used," explained the driver. "He sees Him in his mist. As I said, I am faulty in the dialect."

"Marduk's memory is failing," continued the priest, as if eager to unburden himself of his secret. "He cannot remember His origin. The vast spectacle of his reign, so filled with event, has become blurred in His once-perfect mind. I see Him in my mist but not as my ancestors saw Him. He is now old and enfeebled. But I continue to keep in memory all the glorious attributes of the God, which He Himself has lost."

Burgoine looked down again at the ancient map. We might escape back to the southwest, into Israel. But the border there will be popping. No, it must be the midnight flight out of Bagdad.

The priest of Marduk bowed again before his rock. Then, as if embarrassed for his ragged appearance, he drew himself up straight, taking a pose of dignity as he spoke to the two saboteurs. "To serve the dying God in His death agony is a greater privilege than to have known Him in His days of splendor. The God will die alone, with a single priest to pray for Him." He bowed to the rock and whispered inaudibly.

The driver crept back into his sleeping bag. Almost instantly he was snoring again. Burgoine looked out over the great plain, where the wind was sighing and the hundred thousand faithful had once knelt to the One God. Beyond, to the northwest, was the pipeline.

Mr. Jones's Convention

Searching for something a little different this trip to New York City, Mrs. Woodrow Jones learned that SoHo, with its new shops and art galleries, was not too awfully far from their hotel at the World Trade Center, where her husband was attending a convention. As for Mr. Jones, he liked conventions, but this talk of art galleries made him nervous. It was just the kind of deal Joyce could blow a bundle on.

"Woodrow," she said, "we *need* something special for the conversation nook in the guest room."

"Examine the goods," grumbled Mr. Jones, knowing that when Joyce got this caliber of tone in her voice nothing could stop her.

"I'll make a careful purchase," she said, "just like you always do."

"Talk him down."

"I'll do my best." Mrs. Jones was already preparing to leave, for Mr. Jones had earlier announced his intention of napping for a few hours. But he stopped her now, and drew her to the window. "It's a jungle out there. Be careful."

"Yes, dear," said Mrs. Jones, absently.

Mr. Jones drew the curtains of their hotel room. "Look at that." He pointed to a group of long-robed, bald-headed young men who were coming up the street, beating a drum and singing some crazy nonsense.

"They're religious mendicants, dear." Mrs. Jones was sympathetic toward all heathen faiths as part of her work for the Ladies' Overseas Junior Auxiliary League back home.

"Crackpots," said her husband. From Kennedy Airport to the World Trade Center he'd seen enough to make a decent American sick. "Why don't those guys get a job? I'm telling you, Joyce, it's the crackpots are ruining this country."

"They won't bother me at all, Woodrow. I'll be taking a cab to the art galleries."

Mr. Jones flopped down on the bed, hands behind his head. The thought of his hard-earned money going to some phony art dealer troubled him deeply, but he didn't want to spoil his wife's shopping expedition. "Remember, Joyce, if you don't buy it, nobody else will."

"That's right, Woodrow." Mrs. Jones was no longer listening, as she picked up her purse and walked to the door. "You have a nice nap, dear, and I'll be back with a surprise."

"It'll hang there all year . . . if you don't . . . buy it," muttered Mr. Jones, rolling over on his side.

*   *   *

He woke to a different quality of light coming through the curtains, and the sounds of the city had changed their pitch to that of later afternoon. "Joyce?"

Out. Means nobody's taken her yet. Better if she walks her feet off, so she doesn't drag us off to some night club this evening, with all your sharpers holding out their hands—doormen, waiters, you name it. Last year it was your Latin Quarters.

He went to the window, studied the skyline for a while, and then thought he might take a stroll himself. He splashed on a little cologne, donned a sport jacket, and descended to the street. It was a spring day and, refreshed from his nap, he walked at a good pace from block to block, up the canyons of Manhattan. In less than an hour he found himself peering into the crowded streets of SoHo. The gallery banners swung gently in the spring breeze. Joyce around here somewhere, getting taken to the cleaners.

He strolled through SoHo, and on up into Greenwich Village, a place he'd always wanted to check out. A quick survey showed him it was populated with weirdos, and everything was too expensive. Weirdos, hippies, and crackpots. Wrecking the fabric of society. Going around on roller skates. Send them all to the barber, that's the first step.

Mr. Jones circled slowly, not liking what he saw. Kids, dressed like something from a loony bin, pink hair, wild makeup. Not one of them had a job, he was sure of that. It came from parents letting their guard down. The next thing you know, your children are living in Greenwich Village. Playing bongos.

In the midst of his tour, he realized he'd not eaten for some time; the smell of charcoal burgers drew him to a sidewalk bistro where he sat beneath a striped awning and ordered a burger and a beer.

"Dark or light?"

"Dark or light what?"

"Beer."

"Oh, I gotcha—ah, make it a dark." Had a long walk, I'm dry as a bone. Well, so this is your Village.

He sat, watching the streams of people go by, and noted the frequent absence of brassieres. Quite a town, your New York.

A small group of young people was crossing the street, clad in white and wearing white turbans. Mr. Jones chewed his burger, and shook his head. What they need is a job in the supermarket.

He drank his beer and called for another, and as it was brought to him he noticed the woman sitting a few tables away from him. He sipped his beer slowly and studied her fine, strong features. Now there's a classy doll.

Her eyes were heavily made up, but he liked the effect, and she smoked her cigarette with style. Is she a pro? he wondered, and at that moment she gave him a come-hither smile.

He took a long slow drink of beer, sighting the woman over the edge of his glass. She's a hot number and she's got class. He could tell good clothes when he saw them, he'd formerly been in women's wear.

He turned his head toward the street, but he knew she was still watching him. Then suddenly, he remembered he was married; but he'd forgotten Joyce as if she'd never existed. It goes to show you, he reflected, how things go.

He looked again, into those beckoning eyes, and fumbled in his pocket for a cigarette, wondering what in hell he was going to do next.

She stood up, her body slim, pixyish. Elegant. She walked toward his table as unselfconsciously as a cat, and sitting down beside him said, "I'm out of matches. Do you have one?"

He stared at her dumbly, still unsure of the next move. He wasn't a runaround, he and Joyce had a nice once-a-week relationship. Oh, he gave the secretaries a peck now and then at the Christmas office party, but that was just employee relations, and this—looked like the real thing. The woman was reaching toward him, was taking the lit cigarette from his fingers and applying it to the end of her own. "You look like a lost puppy dog," she said, exhaling smoky words across the table at him.

"Just having a bite."

"Really, darling," said the woman, in a suggestive caliber of tone.

This babe would blow the Green Bush Country Club to bits.

He continued gaping at her, realized his mouth was open and shut it promptly. Her voice came, throatier this time, huskier. "Are you alone?"

"I'm here with my wi— my company. Convention. World Trade Center."

"Yes, I can see how worldly you are," said the woman, running her ankle against his shin.

"Well—" He struggled for words. "I find you—attractive." There, it was out and it felt good and she liked it too, look at her smiling, my lord what a smile, the little girl is dynamite. He felt something move in the pit of his stomach. This one, he suddenly realized, isn't for laughs.

"I live nearby," said the woman.

"Is that so?" Here it comes, Jonesey, and don't forget to ask how much before you examine the goods.

"We might go there for a drink in private."

"We might do just that." He called for the bill. "And the young lady's too." He paid them and checked his bankroll. He had enough to buy any kind of show.

"Thank you," said the woman. "I have some very good bourbon at home."

"OK," said Mr. Jones, standing up. OK, OK.

The sun was setting on the river and he could smell the sea blowing up the street as they walked along. The woman took his arm, pressing her breast into his bicep. This is your real New York afternoon, thought Mr. Jones, the kind where you don't know what's going to happen next. Well, I can take care of myself. Woodrow Jones wasn't born yesterday.

Her building was nothing special, but at least it looked safe. He walked up the stairs behind her, watching her lovely slim hips moving gracefully as she climbed. He thought of Joyce, and what she would say if she knew that at this moment her husband was following a strange dame's rear end up a stairway in the hopes of having a showdown with her.

"Here we are," said the woman, turning down the hall toward a shadowy doorway. He waited as she put her key in the lock, but she turned suddenly and pressed herself against him. Her lips met his and her mouth opened with excitement. She's not a pro, she's just a healthy American woman and I turn her on.

"We'd better go inside," she said softly, and opened the door. He followed her in and was met by a pleasant surprise. It wasn't one of your bohemian dumps, but a bright, tastefully appointed apartment; he knew something about tasteful appointments, he'd been in furniture for years before shifting to women's wear. "Nice place," he said, following her through the kitchen, into the living room.

"I'm glad you like it," she said, and with a flick of her finger set her hi-fi going; another flick lowered the blinds. "I'm sorry if I'm going too fast," she said, "but I start work in an hour."

"I'm pressed for time myself."

"Then I suggest we make the most of it." She came toward him, her hands moved swiftly, and the next thing he knew his pants were in a heap at his ankles. He stepped out of them hurriedly as she removed her blouse. Half-naked she came against him then, and pressed her small firm breasts into the fabric of his shirt. He put his arms around her, crushed her against himself, then slipped his hands down inside her slacks. "Why don't we take these off—" His hands and hers worked together, and she stepped out of her slacks, and stood before him clad only in black panties, and he knew a good quality undergarment when he saw it.

She stepped back, smiled again, then put her hands into the waistband of the lacy thing and lowered it.

Mr. Jones thought he was dreaming, saw the afternoon flash past him like a drowning man sees his life. He struggled for words, found none, caught himself on the edge of nausea.

"What's wrong," said the slender creature, "don't you like me?"

"My god," gasped Mr. Jones, unable to move, unable to think, unable to take his eyes off this incredible being with real tits and a peter.

He felt his mind struggling to shift things into place. The woman was beautiful, soft, classy—*but she had a man's ding-dong!*

She stepped toward him. "I can make you feel much better."

"I'm getting out," said Mr. Jones, reaching for his pants.

"Don't be silly," said the creature, rubbing her breasts against him. "We've come this far—" She stroked his face. "—and there aren't many like me back home."

"Christ in heaven," groaned Mr. Jones. He could not figure out the goods and now he was afraid to examine them. There were the tits alright, a sweet pair. But below, flapping in the air—

Mr. Jones went for his pants.

"Relax, lover," said the creature, lowering herself slowly down, her breasts brushing his thighs, her hands going into his boxer shorts.

Mr. Jones stared desperately at the ceiling. You had to go through with some things, that was all. Or else you look like a tourist.

His boxer shorts went down to his ankles and he felt a kiss on the tip of his peter. *I'm being sucked off,* thought Mr. Jones with alarm. But he had to admit the sensation was not all that bad, was, when you closed your eyes, kind of a nice affair.

Then, with a flash of relief, he realized he wasn't cheating on good old Joyce. This was just a little locker room horseplay.

Just a mild tension reliever.

His knees grew weaker, buckled beneath him, and he sank down into a chair, the creature still clinging to him. Sensations of delight shot up and down his legs. He felt himself being drawn out of himself, weak, giddy. A key executive, reflected Mr. Jones, needs to unwind now and then.

The creature was on top of him, fondling him, causing his hips to raise involuntarily in spasms of joy. Your New York blow job, thought Mr. Jones, thrashing in the chair.

He lay back exhausted, quietly pulling himself together. When he got to his feet, his strange partner handed him his pants. "Thanks," said Mr. Jones, dressing quickly. "Well, I'm off." He headed toward the door.

"Come again, darling," said the creature, letting him out.

Mr. Jones felt it best not to encourage conversation.

He slipped into the hallway and went quickly down the stairs.

*   *   *

"Woodrow, I found the most wonderful painting!"

Mrs. Jones was waiting in their room at the Vista. Triumphantly she pointed to a large canvas propped up on a chair.

Mr. Jones examined it carefully. It appeared to be made of colored mudpies thrown on a bedsheet.

His wife walked back and forth, admiring the canvas from all directions. "Where were you, dear, out for a walk?"

"Yeah, I picked up a bite to eat."

"Was it a nice place?"

"Just one of your Village joints," said Mr. Jones.

Fading Tattoo

Monica and I had known Greta, as you know someone you buy things from—a few pleasantries as we'd paid her for her antiques. She wasn't really an antique dealer, but a trader in bric-a-brac, none of it very old, but she didn't charge much either, as she lacked the conceit necessary for the inflated pricing one finds along the New England coastline in summer.

"I can't sleep nights," she said to me. She was thin, with her gray hair frizzed out, and her eyes had deep circles under them.

"I know a good method," I said. "A hypnotist gave it to me." Greta's watery eyes showed interest toward this exotic technique. "You count backwards to yourself—*ninety-nine, deep asleep, ninety-eight, deep asleep,* and when you start to drift, you say *sleep now.*"

"I'll try that," said Greta, then added, "I get up in the middle of the night and have a cup of coffee."

I suggested that might make it harder to fall back to sleep and that she substitute hot milk, but Greta swore by a cup of coffee in the middle of the night. However, the next time I saw her she told me she'd been counting backwards and had gotten some sleep, which pleased us both.

On the visit following that, we were greeted by her husband, a little man who, like many country people, either forgot or refused to wear dentures, which gave a simpleton's flavor to his speech.

Monica asked him the price of a bookcase, a fine oak piece with sliding glass doors. They used it to store afghans, which Greta crocheted herself, and it was never for sale but we always asked, just in case. Her husband looked at it now, and we could see the wheels turning. Would we finally own it, after all? I was ready to pay a considerable price, if only because we'd waited so long.

"Ninety dollars," he said, with determination, and we tried to restrain ourselves a bit in saying we'd buy it, at once, but I could not help wondering where Greta would put her afghans now.

I then found a ridiculous incense burner, shaped like a roly-poly little turbaned Hindu smoking a hubble-bubble, his mouth a round hole through which the smoke would come out—so that went onto the counter in front of Greta's husband, who wrapped it in newspaper; he was quite roly-poly himself and in his own way a miniature, for he was old and shrinking, I suppose, and had, like my little Hindu, been staring into space when we entered the shop.

Monica had by this time found a strange pair of pink table lamps, from the thirties. "I'll light them for you," said Greta's husband, and we handed them over, onto his counter. He plugged them in and turned the switches; the upright cylinders of pink glass glowed. "They're from the depressed era. They go in the bedroom."

Monica and I made a few obligatory rationalizations for this nonsensical purchase, and Greta's husband began to wrap the lamps in newspaper. I noticed a tattoo on his arm, its edges obliterated by time; I angled my head this way and that, and then realized it was a woman's face in profile. "That's an old tattoo."

He looked down at the fuzzy face on his forearm. "Fifty years I've had that thing and never could get rid of it. My wife always gave me trouble about it, all the time we been married. I lost her last week."

The shop seemed to alter itself around him, a collection that would grow no more; Greta's puzzle was finished and the pieces in the glass cases and on the shelves were all there would be. Her husband sat at the center of it, as in a dead queen's chamber, surrounded by her treasure—old jewelry, knick-knacks, fountain pens, and watches with hands stopped, resting on velvet.

Monica began babbling condolences, her words unimportant, only the tone, that we'd liked Greta, for her decent prices, for how nicely she kept her treasures, for being unable to sleep at night.

"I'm seventy-three," he said. "She was ten years younger. I never expected to be sittin' here like this." He looked around him in the shop. I was looking at the soft-edged tattoo, of a woman's fading face; Greta hadn't liked it but somehow it was her, there on his arm.

"I see her everywhere," he said. "I even had to turn my bed around." He spoke from his stool behind the counter, his toothless gums spraying out his poetry. "I went fishin' yesterday, but I had to come back in. I could see her there, sittin' in the boat. We done everything together, huntin', fishin', you name it."

He'd gotten out a cardboard box, and was laying our pink bed-lamps into it. "You don't do a lot of things you should have done." He looked up at me. "I never had a pit'cher made of her. Snapshots, yes, but not a real pit'cher. That's what you want, a real pit'cher, so you can have her right there in front of you . . . "

His round paunch pressed up against the counter as he placed the lamps gently side by side in the box. "The government said she'd be gettin' her social security check now, seein' as she turned sixty-three, but it turns out they just give two hundred dollars for the burial and nothin' more." He looked up at us. "It don't seem right, with Greta havin' paid into it all her life."

He picked up the roly-poly Hindu dreamer and placed him on top of the lamps. "She was a wonderful worker. Work, work, work." He pointed at the oak case we'd just bought. "All those africans are hers, stitched every one of them. She could copy anything. I've seen her countin' the stitches in something and then she'd sew the same thing up herself." He sewed the counter with his stubby

fingers, then stopped, looked at us. "You'll want a receipt
. . ."

He took out a pad and a pen. "I'm not much at writin'.
Figures, yes, I can add them up, but writin' never come
easy to me. Greta always took care of that." He handed
the pen to Monica. "I been practicin' now though. I go at
it at night—" His hand labored through the air. *"Cup.
Saucer.* And you can read it. But if someone's in the shop
and I get the least bit nervous, it all just goes right out of
my head. Look here—" He leafed through the receipt
pad, pointing at a number of legible pages. "Customers
wrote those up. Now here's one of mine—" He chuckled
softly. "You'd never know what's writ there, would you
. . ."

"Like a doctor's prescription," said Monica, and I
wished she hadn't said it, but he didn't seem to mind. He
was done with doctors for now. "Dealers especially, they
need a clear receipt, so they just write their own."

Monica was writing ours, though we didn't need it,
clear or otherwise, but it was ritual, to be made in the old
queen's chamber, and I too seemed to see her there,
watching over him, through her careful arrangement of
old photo albums, postcards, and ivory fans.

We made our goodbyes and walked to the door, leaving the roly-poly little man at his counter, where he
would stare into space, seeking in the shop for a whisper
he alone might hear. With wet gums he would answer,
and Greta would hear a young man speaking, from long
ago, with sparkling teeth and brand-new tattoo.

Victory
at North Antor

Paddling students was the rule at North Antor High School. The instruments of punishment were manufactured by students in wood shop under the guidance of their teacher, Hammerhead Hanson. Mr. Hanson's standards were high; each paddle must be of hardwood, with a finely tooled handle and plenty of heft in the weight. These crafted paddles were then distributed to the other teachers at North Antor, and used accordingly.

Shrimp Spondoni, a student of Hammerhead Hanson, was presently engaged in making a paddle to be used against his fellow students. He did not like the idea, but being only four foot eleven inches tall he had other things to worry about, such as staying four foot eleven.

The smell of wood shop gave him pleasure, and he liked the smooth finish he was putting on the paddle. But the soul of the instrument made him uneasy. It would seek him out, like a heat-sensing weapon, and he would get it in the ass.

Working beside him was his friend Dick Fontana, Basketball Dick, tall, lean, top scorer in the league, a guy who was going somewhere, in Shrimp Spondoni's view. He himself was going nowhere. After graduating from manual trades, he'd know how to make tie racks and paddles, would be able to wire a doorbell and hook up a toilet, and be qualified to apprentice to some tradesman. Since all the apprentice positions went to the sons of union men, he'd get a job shoveling shit.

But Basketball Dick Fontana would get a scholarship, and would leave North Antor far behind him.

"Put some thought into your work, Spondoni," said Hammerhead Hanson, coming by to check on the progress of the paddle. "That's an important item you're creating. It's going to be Miss Lee's own paddle."

Shrimp Spondoni's cheeks burned at the thought of Miss Lee, the one sexy teacher in North Antor—given to wearing tight skirts, in the habit of crossing her legs beneath her desk, and often seen leaning forward in a loose blouse that opened just enough to be interesting.

"And I'm making her paddle,' said Shrimp, after Hammerhead Hanson walked off.

"Put a heart on it," said Dick Fontana.

"I'll put something on it," said Shrimp, but in fact he only put several coats of shellac on it, so that it gleamed brilliantly, and reflected the lights and faces in Wood Shop 4.

He knew there was something disgusting about what he'd done, about the tender care he'd given to the instrument of destruction—but there was something disgusting about everything at North Antor, and even more disgusting was the fact that he was still only four foot eleven with no sign of further growth in sight. He'd have to stand on a box at graduation ceremonies.

The bell sounded, ending wood shop with Hammerhead Hanson. Shrimp and Dick Fontana moved down the hall to electric shop with Short Circuit Smith. Short Circuit Smith was an ex-wrestler turned teacher. He was not much bigger than Shrimp, but he was tougher than wrapped wire and his use of a paddle had made hard cases like Tony One-Punch Toraldo grit their teeth to keep from crying out as destruction ascended, up through the air, paddle whistling in Short Circuit's hand.

He was seated at his desk, bald and scowling, as his students entered. "How's it going, Mr. Smith," said Shrimp.

"Sit down and shut up."

"Yes sir," said Shrimp, with a smile toward Dick Fontana. He liked putting Short Circuit on, liked inquiring after his health, just to see Short Circuit light up.

The project for the month was the wiring of a large star to be hung on the face of North Antor for Christmas; beside it would go two large electric candles. Shrimp went to his assignment at the tip of one of the golden flames, which took up most of the long shop table. He liked the smells here too, of stripped insulation and bare wire, and of the occasional burnt-out circuit, a faint electrical smell he associated with Short Circuit himself, as if the teacher were wired, right up to his bushy eyebrows.

Short Circuit did not have to tell anyone to begin work. His paddle was prominently displayed on a nail hammered into the wall behind his desk. It hung there, waiting. Beside it hung a more decorative paddle, which his students had wired up with twinkling colored Christmas bulbs and presented to him in years past. Now, as during every Christmas season, it was plugged in and winking at them, red, green, and blue.

Shrimp settled down, lost himself in the work; he enjoyed finding his way through the connections, and would not have minded becoming an electrician's assistant. Instead he would be given the opportunity to work at the button mill, standing on a box at the assembly line, where the noise made you deaf in two years.

"Hey," said Dick Fontana softly, "check it out . . . "

Shrimp looked up. Miss Lee was entering the shop. She was in charge of the Christmas pageant, which would take place beneath Short Circuit's star and candles, and she found the need to talk to him about it for a few minutes every day, which caused the ex-wrestler to leap from his desk, eyebrows riding up and down.

"Yes, Miss Lee, good afternoon. Say good afternoon to Miss Lee, boys."

A rumble of greeting filled the shop, as all eyes fixed on her tweed skirt, blue silk blouse, and high heels. Miss Lee was no spring chicken, and her dark hair was streaked with gray, but she had a body and she liked to flaunt it. Why hadn't somebody married her, that was the question you could waste a lunch hour on. But a cold expression sometimes came over her, making her attractive face go suddenly severe and filling it with impossible demands; she taught math, and she could be cranky about it. Still, she was a good-looking woman and it made you wonder what she was doing at a manual trade zoo like North Antor. There was rumor that she'd taught at a better school and been caught copulating with a fullback on the roof, but this was just a lunch hour story that changed every time you heard it. Nonetheless, there was something odd about Miss Lee—a sexy spinster in a schoolful of garage mechanics.

She crossed the shop floor with long graceful strides, high heels clicking on the tile, her blouse moving gently and suggestively—a special treat for Electric Shop 4, and you knew she knew it, from the faint smile on her lips and the way she seemed not to see anyone, or feel the hungry looks that covered her as she walked past the benches.

Short Circuit led her to the window, and they stood there together, looking out to where the pageant would take place, on a platform being constructed by Hammerhead's junior class. Miss Lee bent over the windowsill, and her skirt rose up revealing thighs enclosed in the soft sheen of stockings. Short Circuit rocked backward on his heels, head swiveling for a better view of the pleasant sight, and before he could stop himself, Shrimp called out, "Five hundred volts, Mr. Smith!"

Short Circuit spun around, eyebrows twitching. He

stared at Shrimp for one long moment, then said, "Take my paddle off the wall."

Fear shot through Shrimp's small frame. No one could drive you home like Short Circuit Smith. This was a man who formerly ran opponents' heads into ring posts. Each day after school he worked out in the gym with dumbbells. He had caused Tony One-Punch to buckle. What's he going to do to me, reflected Shrimp as he walked slowly toward the front of the room and stopped alongside of the hanging paddles. "Which one?" he asked, a stupid smile on his face. He reached for the Christmas paddle, the lights winking gaily at him. "The other one, Spondoni," said Short Circuit Smith, and turned toward his visitor. "Excuse me, Miss Lee, this won't take long."

Shrimp waited, still smiling stupidly as Short Circuit came toward him. "Let's position you just right, Spondoni, for maximum liftoff—"

A few laughs rippled through the shop, and Shrimp understood. He'd be laughing if some other guy was getting it. When you were bent over with your ass on the launch pad, it was funny—until the moment of destruction.

Short Circuit angled him so that he was looking toward Miss Lee, into those soft doe-eyes of hers, so dark and shining. Her gaze was fixed on him, with an expression he couldn't fathom. Was she smiling, just faintly, as Short Circuit prepared him for orbit? Her hips were resting against the windowsill, spreading just a little, tightening her skirt around her, underwear visible through the thin fabric. Her eyelids blinked gently, and he felt the hush descend in the room—Short Circuit was winding up.

CRACK!

Excruciating pain shot through him as he spread forward on the desk and his face contorted. *Just don't give me another one*

CRACK!

He knocked his forehead down on the desk, fighting back the cry that was shooting through him. He twisted sideways and saw Dick Fontana, Dick's eyes cold, rage-filled and fixed on Short Circuit. Shrimp tried to unbend, but his legs were trembling and he couldn't let go of the desk. He looked at Miss Lee, and the same faint smile was still on her lips.

*   *   *

That night Shrimp did not sit down, but it didn't matter, for he spent the time on his feet shouting with the rest of the school, as Dick Fontana scored thirty points against Winfield Academy. "Go, Dick, go!" Shrimp held to the balcony railing, shaking his fist and calling to Fontana, who was running all over the fancy Dans from Academy, hotshots who were going to become lawyers, doctors, and other things that no one from North Antor would have a chance at—except Dick Fontana. There were big-time scouts in the gymnasium tonight, everybody knew it. "Go, Dick, ram it down their throat, baby! Show them what you can do!"

Dick Fontana turned in the air, the ball arcing from his

fingertips. Shrimp leaned over the railing, putting his will into the shot, helping the ball on its way.

"Shrimp, we don't want to lose you—" Tony One-Punch drew him back, as the ball snapped smoothly through the net.

"Way to go, Dick, way to go, baby!"

When the game was over, Shrimp swarmed with the crowd outside in the winter darkness. The Academy bus was waiting and the students of North Antor were rocking it back and forth, jeering their defeated rivals. The Academy players sat coolly inside, with their cheerleaders to console them. Tony One-Punch, carried away by victory, drilled a punch into the bus window, spidering the glass, behind which the Academy star center sat, still just staring coolly down, his lips quietly saying, "You're an animal."

"The animals kicked your ass," snarled Tony, and wound up again. Shrimp pushed in closer to the action, for the Winfielders weren't pushovers, and he might be needed; he'd developed some good low moves necessary to someone his size. As he went into his fighting crouch, a hand came on his shoulder. He spun around, ready to bite, and found himself looking up at Dick Fontana.

They pulled away from the crowd, onto a quieter street, and continued down it, the noise from the gymnasium fading behind them. "You had a great game," said Shrimp. "You drove those fruits through the floorboards."

"They were easier than I thought they'd be."

"They weren't easy, they were tough. But you were a

whole lot tougher. The way you went up on that guy—" Shrimp went into a jump shot, springing his four foot eleven inches into the air, so that Dick could see what had gone on tonight. Shrimp came down bouncing, and felt twinges all over his backside. He rubbed it tenderly, across the welts Short Circuit Smith had raised.

"How's your assbone?"

"I'll be standin' for a while. Did you see the way he drilled me? The sonofabitch practically ran across the room."

"He came all the way around on you."

"I'll come all the way around on him. I'll drop a tv set on his head from fifty up some night. He won't get away with paddling me."

"They always get away with it," said Dick Fontana softly.

"Short Circuit was showin' off for Miss Lee. And she stood there smilin' while he blasted me."

"She's hot stuff."

"She's a hot piroshki sandwich. I'll get her someday too."

They walked along the Strip, where the serious drinking was done in a string of smoky dives, neon buzzing outside them, advertising the local beer. Then the streets grew darker, leading to the railroad tracks and the warehouses, where rows of tractor trailers were parked. The smell of the river was near, green and polluted by the mill where Shrimp figured he'd be working after graduation. "I hear there were scouts at the game, you hear that?"

"I heard, but nobody came to talk to me."

"They will, baby. They'll be around. You'll be playin' in the Ivy League."

They crossed the river on the rickety slats that formed the walkway over slow water carrying a green moon on its back. On the other side of the bridge was their neighborhood, mostly coal miners' houses, flooded by the river every spring. They walked through the dimly lit thoroughfare, the moon reflected now in a series of water-filled potholes. Through the windows, Shrimp saw the familiar sights—wallpaper peeling off, bare light bulbs hanging in the middle of a room where kids were screaming and a radio was blasting.

Dick's house was falling apart, the shingles cracked and peeling off, the front porch sagging toward the ground. Mrs. Fontana was in the kitchen, a baby on her shoulder, as she stirred pots on the stove. A line of wash hung behind her in the kitchen, and Shrimp saw a pair of basketball trunks, North Antor–colored.

Dick pushed through a rusty creaking gate. "See you tomorrow. Sit down easy."

Shrimp continued along the muddy sidewalk. "You creamed them, baby. You're on the way. All-state center."

He walked on, along paths he knew in the dark, from yard to yard. He moved quickly, easily, small figure crouched as he tunneled through an open hedge. The victory of the evening was in him, the screams and cheers still sounding; the swift motion on the court was in his own step now, as he leapt from the hedge, spun, shot an invisible ball through the air. "We creamed them, baby, we blew them away."

He was in his own yard now, beside a rusty old Dodge that'd been there since before he was born; he moved past the derelict vehicle, through a tangle of dead weeds and grass. The two-room little house ahead of him was dark except for the glow of a tv screen. He went through the back door and found the old man on a couch in the kitchen, toes sticking out of tattered socks. A cloud of smoke wreathed his head and a bottle of gin was on the floor beside him. "How's it goin'."

"OK," said Shrimp. "Dick creamed Academy."

"Atta boy," said the old man, and poured himself another drink.

*   *   *

Shrimp climbed up the stairs of the special bus the school had chartered, one of several that were pointed toward the capital for the state championship game. The team had gone on ahead, had been there a whole day already, to have some practice on the playoff court. Shrimp's bus held the North Antor band, the cheerleaders, and anyone else who could squeeze in. Room was made for Shrimp in the back, and he sat down, holding his lunch bag. "We'll be comin' back with the trophy," he said to his compatriots—Tony One-Punch, Jimmy Jaboola, and Frankie Plunger, who'd made certain they too were riding with the cheerleaders.

The cheerleaders led the bus in singing the school songs, and they sang all the way, hour after hour; Shrimp felt a magical excitement, felt victory in the air—they were going to be the state champs. Tony One-Punch and Frankie Plunger danced in the aisle, pulling the captain of the cheerleaders from her seat and spinning her around. Her skirt flew up, her pink panties showed, and everyone shouted hurray. Shrimp joined the dance, tried to get his head under her skirt, and she laughed, pushing him away. "We're gonna win!" yelled Shrimp, rolling down the aisle in a ball for her. "We're gonna win big!"

* * *

The Palestra was mobbed, every seat in the house filled, and every exit crowded with spectators. North Antor was just coming onto the floor, and Shrimp felt that it was himself out there on the floor in shiny costume, under the big lights, the focus of the whole state on this North Antor team which had come out of nowhere to challenge the big powerhouse schools. They'd beaten them all, with just one more to go—one last victory and they'd be kings.

"Give us an N, give us an O—"

The cheerleaders were on the floor, waving their pompoms, and North Antor was running through their warm-up weave, ball snapping smoothly from hand to hand. "Dick's looking good, he's on tonight, look at that hook shoot."

"Here come the—"

Here come the cats from Phillie, man. Look at the size of those motherfuckers.

The championship team from the other half of the

state sailed down the court, black bodies tall and fast, ball flying between them. Their center leapt at the net and jammed the ball down through it with the force of a cannonshot.

*   *   *

Shrimp's bus got back home at midnight, emptying at the front gates of North Antor. Shrimp walked on from there, cutting down through the coal company's vast yard, past the great breaker in shadow against the moon-lit sky. The huge coal piles were dark hills, through whose valleys he passed, threading his way along unmarked trails. The coal company faced the river and he crossed it by the railroad bridge, from tie to tie over the open rushing water.

The neighborhood was dark now, the only light coming from Dick Fontana's house, and he saw Dick inside, sitting alone at the kitchen table. He tapped on the window and Dick got up and came out onto the porch. Shrimp looked up into the tall center's tired face.

"Fuck it, man."

They sat on the sagging porch railing and looked out toward the river. Beyond it was the coal breaker, with the moon attached to the top of it like a night-shift light, illuminating the long chutes. "The scouts talked to me after the game. I got three offers."

"Way to go."

Dick rocked back on the railing, a long slow breath escaping him. "That center of theirs was something else."

"Hey, you rammed a whole bunch of shots down his throat."

"He rammed a whole bunch more down mine."

"The guy was a freak. A regular freak of nature." Shrimp lowered himself from the railing. "He buys his clothes at a store for giraffes."

"He'll make it to the pros."

"For one reason only, his old man was a pogo stick." Shrimp paced along the railing. "Did they make you a money offer?"

"Money and a car."

"So you can kiss this town goodbye." Shrimp stepped down off the porch. "I'll see you in Miss Lee's class tomorrow. We'll snap her garters for her."

He left Dick standing on the porch, figured he wanted to be alone now, to think things through, to consider his future, and forget the defeat. But we almost made it. We were right there at the top.

He walked through the backyards of the neighborhood, past the silent, weather-beaten old buildings. The defeat was still with him, and it was real, while victory was now fading back into dreamland. They called us the Cinderella team. How about that. The Cinderella team.

He knew now that they'd never been meant to win it, that the dream had been beyond their reach right from the start, and it felt like his own fate had been bound up with the Cinderella team, that if they'd won he wouldn't have had to go to work in the pillow factory and breathe feathers all day. But North Antor had to lose, and he would have to breathe chicken feathers and itch all over his body for the next fifty-five years. Because that was the way things worked out in the real world. But he couldn't help wondering about those other people, the ones for whom the dream world was the place they laid claim to. That, finally, was the other side of the tracks.

He went over the low fence, into his own backyard. The house was dark except for the glow of the tv screen, showing its usual bent picture, with everybody's head two feet long. He walked in and found the old man on the couch, covered in newspapers.

"How's it goin'."

"We lost."

"Atta boy." The old man lifted his bottle and drank a little toast.

*   *   *

A shadow hung over the school, the halls gloomy, voices low. We had it made, thought Shrimp, as he entered Miss Lee's class, the first one of the day. We were Cinderella.

He looked around, saw Tootsie Zonka, captain of the cheerleaders, and her eyes were red from crying. He'd rolled down the aisle of the bus for her just a night ago, and seen her pink panties, but that'd been in dreamland, never to be gotten back. You had one chance for the state championship, and then it was the button mill, the pillow factory, or the sewer works.

"Hey, Tootsie, cheer up, you looked great out there."

She glanced at him and smiled, but her eyes were far

away, still in dreamland, still with what was supposed to
have been—herself carrying the trophy for the whole
school as they held their victory celebration in the North
Antor gym.

Miss Lee entered the room, and paraded to her desk,
skirt whispering as she walked, perfume floating over the
first few rows. Losing the championship meant bodunkus
to her, Shrimp was sure of that; she never went to any of
the games, was only interested in her own sweet self. She
sat down, crossed her legs beneath the desk, and class
began. Shrimp looked at her crossed legs, not really car-
ing much about them today, just looking out of habit. She
was a good-looking old doll, but so what? We had the
state in our hands, had that gleaming trophy in reach. He
saw the trophy in his mind, a clear white pedestal with a
bronze figure on top of it, holding a basketball in the air.
The figure was himself, all four foot eleven inches of him.

"Mr. Spondoni, I asked you a question."

Shrimp looked up from his dream, stared dumbly at
Miss Lee. She had her cranky face on today, the sucking-
lemons one that pursed her lips and put a furrow in her
brow. Her dark eyes were fixed on his, faintly menacing.
He realized, all of a sudden, that he didn't give a shit
what she thought, said, did, expected, or hoped for.

"Did you hear what I said, Mr. Spondoni?"

"No."

"No?" Her eyebrow arched up, her face seemed shel-
lacked, like something made in wood shop class. "It is
your responsibility to listen in this classroom. Do you
know what that means?"

"Yeah, *this.*" He raised his right hand and stuck his middle finger in the air, right under her nose.

She stared in amazement, which matched his own, for he couldn't believe that it was his finger out there wriggling in the air. But then he knew, that's how the trophy looked, with himself on the pedestal, giving the finger.

"Bend over, young man . . . " She dragged him from his seat and shoved him against her desk. Her other hand was reaching out for her paddle, which hung from a nearby hook.

Shrimp looked at it, saw his own work, the handle of the paddle smoothly carved, the face smooth as glass, meant for destruction. But Miss Lee did not really know how to use it. "Gimme your best shot," he said over his shoulder, and then looked at Tootsie Zonka and winked.

He heard Miss Lee winding up, felt himself inside the cloud of her sweet, despised perfume. And then she drilled him, with a force so surprising the tears shot out of his eyes, for himself, for Dick Fontana, for Tootsie, for all of them. "You no-good lousy fucking bitch. *Here!*" His finger was in the air again before he knew it, the trophy figure shining on its pedestal.

The door of the classroom flew open, and standing there, eyes burning like something found in the coal-breaker, was principal Herbert T. Astle, the silver-haired sadist. "I'll handle this, Miss Lee," he said, crossing the room with quick strides.

Shrimp pulled back, eyes darting wildly. Herbert T. Asshole was the undisputed master of the paddle, with a technique far surpassing that of Short Circuit Smith. He ruled the school by means of it and a gold-toothed smile that gave him the look of a cat preparing to chew on a mouse's head. "Bend over, Spondoni," he said, and took the paddle from Miss Lee.

Shrimp felt himself freezing up, rage and courage gone in the presence of the supreme ruler. This was the guy who could send him to a reformatory, and that was not in Shrimp's game-plan.

"He disrupted this class in the most obscene manner," said Miss Lee, voice shaking with anger as she moved closer to the kill.

"He'll think twice about it in future, I assure you of that." Herbert T. Asshole shoved a hand in the middle of Shrimp's back. "Hold it precisely there, Spondoni . . . "

"You hold it," said a soft voice from the back of the room.

Herbert T. Asshole spun around, and then his eyes narrowed. "Sit down, Fontana."

Dick remained standing, relaxed but seeming to be ready, the way he looked at the beginning of a game, when he was about to jump for the ball against an opposing center.

Herbert T. Asshole walked down the aisle toward him, slowly, his own voice soft now. "I can break you and your future, with one phone call."

Fontana gazed at him, eyes expressionless, his body still seeming to be at ease, yet the tension was there, the thing that could suddenly spring up at you, tower over you, drive a basketball down your throat. He took a step toward Herbert T. Asshole, and the principal stepped backward, his voice getting suddenly higher. "I'll suspend you for this——" He continued backing up, collided with Miss Lee's desk; the paddle, still in his hand, struck her flower vase and sent it to the floor where it shattered, water and roses spilling out of it. Shrimp stepped aside as the water trickled past his shoe. He looked at Fontana, and Dick's face was calmer than he'd ever seen it, as if this gold-toothed fiend jabbering at him was just a stranger on a street corner, past whom one simply walked. Dick walked, and Shrimp walked with him.

"You won't get away with this!" Herbert T. Asshole ran after them toward the door. They stepped through, and the principal whirled around, back toward the class, where Tootsie Zonka was standing up, and Tony One-Punch, and Frankie Plunger. The whole class stood up and walked out of the room, in a quiet, solemn march.

*   *   *

Shrimp left the pillow factory, arms itching up to the elbow. It was a winter day, the air crisp and clear. He walked along the river to the corner store and bought a paper, turning immediately to the sports page. He found the write-up on the big college game, and saw Dick Fontana's picture in a little square frame. "Go get 'em, baby." Shrimp folded the paper under his arm, and walked on.

A Man Who Knew
His Birds

Meechum swung his binoculars up. The forest veil played its deception, but among the leaves the rust of a flickering tail went up and down. Meechum pressed a button on his recorder. "Hermit thrush," he said softly.

"Tuck, tuck, tuck," said the thrush.

It was routine work. After these few last observations, he'd be heading on, following the migration, south to Guatemala.

"Kit, kit," said the wren.

"Queedle, queedle," said the jay.

Meechum stalked ahead, mentally composing the pages of his textbook. In his imagination it was ornamented with creeping vines and tendrils, but in the museum edition it would, of course, be a straightforward work.

"Beep, beep," said the woodcock.

"Smack, smack," said the thrasher.

The forest gave way to an old field, flat except for some grass-grown rocks, piled by a farmer a half-century ago. Meechum moved along the edge of the meadow, threading a line between forest and field, recording, sorting, arranging, cataloging the sights and sounds.

At the meadow's end, he stopped, cupped his hands around his mouth and gave a sharp staccato call. Calls were his specialty; he could lure birds along, playing on their instincts with perfect certainty of the outcome.

"Queedle, queedle," answered the jay on cue a moment later, to confirm the theory of irreversible drives sealed by mechanical fates.

A breeze played over the meadow. Grass and flowers bent and swayed. Insects and birds fluttered along, but only one mind was at work, and it was Meechum's. *For only in man,* went the text of his book, *are the powers of intellect freed. Man alone,* the paragraph concluded, *has broken the bars of instinct.*

A few illuminated vines and leaves wound around this, and its author stalked on, listening to the marvelous but mindless machine on all sides of him—queedling, tuck-tucking, smack-smacking. Meechum filed the bird-calls, with that easeful certainty of the expert, with a peculiar sort of thunking sensation in his brain, of material going where it was supposed to.

He walked along, noting the peculiarities of terrain, expecting and finding nests exactly where they should be. A pair of eggs was revealed in a nest deftly hidden, not in a tree but in a certain kind of ground cover Meechum knew well; finding the eggs there filled him with sadness almost, for the poor birds would always and everlastingly lay their eggs that way, and an intelligent investigator would always find them. The poor simple creatures were slaves to instincts that occasionally seemed pitiful. He disguised the ground nest again. No, he said to himself, there is no freedom here, free as we may think the birds are. And it is always the same—they are mechanical creations.

As for their fabulous singing, reflected Meechum, it too is instinctual and predictable down to the last note. The beauty of evensong is an ancient recording, the same now as it was ten thousand years ago—unchanging, caught in unrelenting sameness. A shame, in a way, but that is blind nature's style. Man alone has been freed, and man alone rules.

And Meechum felt that man's sentimental projections concerning birdsong would ultimately die, and be banished by a more accurate and scientific view of the matter. No, birdsong was not inspired nor was it the poetry that emotional fools made of it. It was—code. And he, Meechum, was master of the code.

"Zwee, zwee, zwee," said the blue warbler.

"Pee-wee? Pee-wee?" asked the flycatcher.

And then: *"Who-cooks-for-you, who-cooks-for-you . . ."*

Extraordinary, thought Meechum. He's 1500 miles off the beam.

And then: *"No-hope, no-hope . . ."*

Meechum could not have been more stunned if he'd

walked into a wall. A white-winged and an Inca dove, here?

Fifteen hundred miles off the beam?

He entered the brush, his excitement growing, the fading afternoon tingling with discovery as he switched on his tape recorder.

"Who-cooks-for-you, who-cooks-for-you . . . "

Marvelous! He went down on all fours and moved deeper into the brush. There was a faint rustling off to the side, as of a large animal circling, but what he sought was much smaller, much more delicate, would be holding to the ground, just ahead. Carefully, gently, he moved one branch aside, and then another.

The parted veil revealed—nothing at all.

He brought himself up closer, like an inchworm. He'd make identification in a moment more, of course, he could never fail on something like this.

"Howdy . . . "

The voice spun him around, crazily, as if the forest floor were a rug that'd been pulled out from underneath him. Meechum stared across the little clearing, in which he'd never ever heard a single human sound, and now, at a crucial time like this, on the brink of an extraordinary sighting—

"You lost?" A grizzled old local was coming toward him, hat on sideways, a demented grin on his face. Drunk, thought Meechum, an old drunk . . .

"Please," said Meechum softly, "there's a bird in there." He pointed toward the bushes.

"Well, flush the bugger out!" The codger took off his cap, rushed at the bushes, and started beating on them.

"No!" Meechum grabbed him by the arm. The old yokel was light as a feather and Meechum easily pulled him back.

"You go at 'er strong, don'cha . . . " The old drunk cackled and spat a stream of tobacco juice into the leaves where the rare doves were, or had been.

"Please," said Meechum again, speaking slowly, as if to an idiot. "I'm doing field work. I've made an important sighting of a wind-drifted vagrant . . . "

The man squinted toward the leaves. "Pair of pigeons?"

Meechum's heart sank. "Yes, are they yours?"

"Brought 'em all the way from Mexico," said the man, proudly straightening his hat.

"I see," said Meechum, crestfallen, the moment gone, the day over. "The doves are pets."

"I was out there workin' . . . " The old man smelt faintly of fish. The ocean wasn't far; he must be a fisherman. ". . . I seen them pigeons and heard 'em talking 'mongst themselves—"

"Yes," said Meechum glumly, putting his microphone away for the day, ". . . and you brought them back with you."

"—goin' *who-cooks-for-you, who-cooks-for-you*—"

Meechum's hand stopped, with the microphone still in it. Automatically, he clicked it on again. "What did you say?"

"I said, *who-cooks-for-you, who cooks-for-you.*" The old cod's mouth wrinkled up mischievously, producing the most perfect dove call Meechum had ever heard.

"No-hope, no-hope," continued the codger in the same

expert tones, his toothless gums shaping the delicate sound. Then, seeing the confusion on Meechum's face, he burst into laughter.

It took Meechum's brain a second to catch up to the wild high-pitched laugh, but his file-system was whirling, the laughter familiar, incredibly so.

Fulmaris glacialis, observed Meechum, as the correct file-drawer opened in his mind, and then closed again a moment later with a thunking sensation, of material going where it was supposed to—laughter of the Arctic seabird, south to Newfoundland, also northern Eurasia—*but produced by an old nut in the forest.*

"Yessir," said the codger, "I brung them pigeons here alright, and turned 'em loose. Along with all the rest." He looked at Meechum, slapped his thigh and started laughing again—weird, shifting, kaleidoscopic screeching. Meechum experienced a succession of thunks in his head, more drawers opening and closing as the old fisherman's laughter ranged quickly through bird families from the eastern Atlantic to the Indian Ocean.

Meechum heard brown boobys, painted storks, red jungle fowls, the great hummingbird of the Andes, and a mousebird of Africa; the forest seemed to fill with toucans, trogons, wood hoopoes, nightjars, honey guides, and common cuckoos. He heard, distinctly, parrots, parakeets, puffins, and a razor-billed auk. Meechum turned his recorder nervously, on, off, on again.

"Yessir, there are more birds in these parts than a feller might think," cackled the old reprobate. "Well, they keeps the bugs away, right? Eh?" He cackled again, and poked Meechum good-naturedly in the ribs with his bony finger.

Meechum teetered, and pitched backward.

"What's wrong?" asked the old loony, as Meechum sank down heavily on a moss-covered stump. "You feelin' alright? You sure you ain't lost?"

"No . . . " stammered Meechum, feeling as if he'd just bounced from breeding ground to breeding ground, halfway round the earth.

The old zany laughed again, then gave a low *"hoooo, hooo, hoooo."* He looked at Meechum. "You know what that is?"

"Spruce grouse."

"We call 'em fool hens," said the old man, and cackled again, as at the funniest joke in the world. A long series of calls came from him then, in rapid succession. Meechum followed each of them, his mind going though its regular cataloging, a lifetime's training at work.

"Queer-a-chi-queer, queer-a-chi-queer . . . " The old man was dancing, shaking his pants legs, rattling off calls with mad glee. Meechum closed his eyes, saw the Dry Tortugas, then a soft Brazilian moon. He opened his eyes, saw the codger a few feet from him, toothless gums beating. A green warbler had landed in his hat.

Meechum pointed his microphone instinctively, but it was not the warbler who sang into it, but rather the old man, and the song was that of some fantastic mockingbird whose repertoire was music from a thousand forests, a million lakes, and the seven seas.

Meechum's mind whirled, faster than any tape recorder, from call to call, his information bank lighting up madly as the old sailor cackled and cawed, twittered and cooed, clicked and whistled.

If he publishes, thought Meechum, I'm ruined.

This painful thought was quickly submerged, for Meechum found it impossible to think with such an awesome medley of bird-calls filling his brain. He wanted to rise and go, wanted to find the path to the road and drive away, but he was fastened to the stump, filing, cataloging, filing some more, as the old loony danced, arms akimbo, calling, calling, calling, in a Babel of bird-tongues, the warbler still sitting in his hat.

Meechum's mouth hung open, his eyes glazing over. He was imprisoned, he was being called.

No call was left out, from jungle to mountaintop. How? his free mind would have cried, but it was no longer free. Meechum sat like a toadstool, like a tree-ear, listening.

"Titi-ri-titi-ri, titi-ri-titi-ri . . . "

The old man flapped his elbows, cocked his head, scuffled his feet. Meechum blinked mechanically, seeing a dejected hunched plover on the Arctic tundra, then a spasmodic running wagtail on Spanish ground—yet the only real bird present was the warbler in the old codger's hat. The warbler looked at Meechum.

Its little black eyes filled with an expression Meechum had never seen before. The warbler turned, first this way, then that, to stare at him. His own brain was numbed, netted, imprisoned by song, and the warbler was saying, in illuminated thought framed round with vines and tendrils, *Birds alone know the meaning of song.*

Meechum closed his eyes. Texts and guides were fluttering in his head, page after page, the pages blurring like wings in flight. He saw an immense wheeling formation, heard its magnificent call, an immensity of wingbeats fluttering through his nerves.

He forced his eyes open, expecting to see an evening sky filled with birds, but there were only the pines, and a crazy old coot, hopping toward the brush, with a warbler in his hat. Twittering, cheeping, cawing, the old man disappeared, and a moment later the forest was still.

Meechum rose from his stump, and listened. There was a faint klee-klee-klee from afar.

"Merlin," he said softly into his microphone. *"Labrador south to Nova Scotia."*

A faint whisper of wings came out of the pines and the shadow of the little Merlin-hawk glided silently by.

Letter to a Swan

Lake Zurich glistened, reflecting the first sun for many days. Spring was late and all Europe seemed unseasonably cold. DuJohn sat at the stern of the ferry, huddled in his jacket, staring down at a mottled swan on the water; as the ferry approached, the great bird raised its wings and flapped away, long legs cutting a narrow wake in the water, toward the shore. The ferry followed, turning landward to Küsnacht.

He joined Marie at the gangplank; they walked down to the dock and on into the little town. A two-lane highway had to be traversed, but beyond it were the hills, through which was woven a network of small streets. The houses were all marked with the craftsmanship of Old Europe, which spoke through the heavy wooden doors, the iron hinges, the careful work of the tiled roofs and eaves. Flowing down from the hills was a wide stream, descending between the houses over tiers of stone to the lake. Pedaling across a narrow bridge above the water was an elderly gentleman on a bicycle. DuJohn stopped him, asking him for directions to the cemetery, to the grave of Carl Jung. The man shook his head, and pedaled on.

"We can ask there," said Marie, pointing to an old church and the cleric's house beside it. But the bell went unanswered, echoing within an empty house.

They walked back to the stone bridge spanning the stream. He looked up it toward the next bridge, where two men stood gazing at the river. "We can ask them."

"Look," said Marie, bending to retrieve a flower from the sidewalk. It was a magenta orchid, wrapped in cellophane and still fresh. Green ferns surrounded it and the arrangement was gathered at the base into a pointed stem. She looked up and down the street, but whoever had dropped the flower had disappeared.

"It's for Jung," said DuJohn.

"Yes," she said, "I guess it must be. But we've got to find the cemetery first."

He turned back toward the bridge. The two men who'd been watching the water were gone, and for a moment he wondered if they'd been apparitions and the flower their work. Hadn't Jung been called the Hexenmeister of Zurich?

"The town's not that big," he said. "If we keep wandering we're bound to come to it."

Marie led the way, into the kind of winding little street

she liked best, a narrowness that spoke of horse-drawn carriages. DuJohn stalked the elusive feeling with her, of the venerable spirit hiding in old passages. It showed its gray beard momentarily and moved on, from lane to lane, promising to reveal more, only to vanish again. The labyrinth led higher into the hills, where the stone pavement ended and the houses fell away. The forest was ahead of them now.

They climbed a wide path rising gently through pines and birch. Beside it the stream still meandered, down through the woods. The smell of pine brought DuJohn the feeling he always had in forests, of someone following close behind him—a sprite from the earth or a tree gnome. He'd cut a lot of trees down in his time, and once, on a spring day in the north woods, he'd apologized to a great stand of spruce that he and some other loggers were cutting through. A childlike voice had replied to him, *Man is not our father, our father is the sun.*

Now, at the top of the wooded hill, he rested on a carpet of pine needles, and stared up through the branches. *Man is not our father, our father is the sun.* It had been a gentle voice, and he'd thought of the trees as dancers then, exotics performing for their father the sun—root dancers, limb dancers, the aspen the most delicate of the dancers, and the apple striking poses of great mystery.

He put his arm around Marie. " *'There is none like thee among the dancers.'* It's by Ezra Pound. I wish I could remember the rest. I've often wondered why I can't memorize poetry. I practiced that piece of Pound's every day for a year and I've forgotten it completely."

"That's the sort of mind you have," said Marie, from the crook of his arm.

"There have been occasions when I could have come out with an appropriate line of poetry and impressed everyone."

"Thank goodness you didn't."

"I suppose it's a blessing in a way." He closed his eyes and said again softly, "There is none like thee among the dancers."

The sun went in and out of the clouds, the forest alternating between gray and gold, settling finally on gray, which brought the wind. He felt the rumble of thunder moving in the earth, and they stood, and continued on. When the hilltop revealed its view, it was of a giant mechanical crane and the steel skeleton of a high rise. The great arm of the crane swung along the hillside. *See Europe before it turns into Cleveland,* a friend had told him.

The high-rise side of the mountain took them to a steep winding street, and here the houses did not whisper of antique spirits. The drives, the gardens, the nameplates spoke frankly of sound investments. On one of the gates was a forbidding sign: *Warnung—von dem Hund.*

"Beware of the dog," said DuJohn. "There he is." They looked over the shrubbery and saw a miniature schnauzer on the sidewalk. He was lost in a dream, staring into the grass. They stepped closer and he remained oblivious of them, involved in quiet doggy mysteries. The memory of a bone? wondered DuJohn, deciding it probably wasn't, that it probably had to do with things less specific than bones, things so vague and fleeting that only a half-sleeping dog could begin to comprehend them.

"Mein Herr Hund," said DuJohn softly, and began writing the hund a letter: *We saw your sign and ver vundering if you are der famous vunderhund. Knowing you are busy vunderhunding your premises and trusting this short note vill not distract you, ve are, faithfully, your admiring public.*

They walked on and, after the first bend, the road down the hillside turned so suddenly steep that their legs were forced into awkward steps, like two wooden puppets. But other footsteps sounded behind them, and they were swiftly passed by a young man carrying a briefcase, who glided loosely down the grade as if he had wheels in his feet.

"He understands this hill," said DuJohn.

"We should have asked him directions to the cemetery."

"We'd have broken his stride. He's like those Tibetan mailmen who can run for days in a trance. It's forbidden to speak to them."

They rounded the bend; the walking man was far below already. DuJohn tried to loosen his own stride, unsuccessfully. One has to train, he reflected, learn the fine points. He crouched, trying to find the natural downward flow, saw a door opening in a townhouse ahead of him and quickly straightened, not wishing to look like a demented American.

A woman appeared in the doorway, leading her two children. They walked to the drive and got into a new Mercedes. As she slipped behind the wheel, the woman glanced at DuJohn. She was nearing middle age with grace, her hair pulled back in a severe and flattering line, her body trim. But DuJohn caught something in the glance, or was it in the air of the house, like a sigh that escaped from every pore of her graceful life. He suspected she did not know how to glide down this hill either.

At the bottom of the hill, they entered the main street of Küsnacht again. The shops had now closed, their windows shuttered; he saw the open doorway of a newspaper office and went to ask directions there, and found in the outer hall a large street plan of Küsnacht. There were two cemeteries, green areas marked with crosses, one at each end of town. He carefully traced the line they had to take, stepped outside, got his bearings, and started off. A few blocks later none of the streets bore the names he sought. "Well, either way we go is correct," he said. "We're bound to find one cemetery or the other. How's our flower holding up?"

He looked into the fragrant interior of the blossom, but it was not the flower it had been at sunrise, its life seeping slowly away.

They walked on, expecting the cemetery to appear at every turning. It shouldn't be this far, thought DuJohn. I've gotten turned around and we're headed for the cemetery at the other end of town. Well, process of elimination. We know Jung's buried in Küsnacht.

"Do the street signs look familiar yet?" asked Marie.

"No, I don't know where we are."

"We can ask that woman," she said, nodding toward the corner of the next block, where a stout *Frau* was pushing a wheelbarrow along her sidewalk.

Instead, he led them toward a wooded area below, that might mark the far end of Küsnacht, where the cemetery should be. They found railroad tracks. He sat down with a sigh on the embankment and Marie sat beside him, the flower in her lap.

His legs were starting to tire, and the day was turning colder. A shadow of complaint started to cast itself across his mind—*I'm worn out and we're wandering around like a pair of idiots*—except that he knew the only way to wander around was precisely that way, like an idiot. Then the enchantment had a chance.

But it would have no chance at all if he started grumbling about tired feet. A letter was in order, to the first spirit of the day: *Dear Mottled Swan, we saw your glorious mottled plumage and excellent pink bill, and shall always think of it with vunder and admiration. Respectfully, your secret friends.*

"Maybe if we tried this path," he said, standing. They followed the path, which ended in a backyard. "This isn't the way to the cemetery."

"Maybe," said Marie quietly, "we should ask the woman with the wheelbarrow."

They retraced their steps back to the street, where the *Frau* was tipping a barrow of wet cement into a sidewalk form. There was a cemetery in this direction, she informed them, but it was on the top of the hill, very far. "It's the old cemetery. I do not recommend walking there. Try the new cemetery, that way," she said, pointing in the direction of the newspaper office, from which they'd started.

They walked on as instructed, but DuJohn was certain the woman was wrong. "Jung's buried in the old cemetery on the hill. I'm sure of it. The commanding view. That's Jung's style."

"But she said we should try the other one, the new one."

"Yes, but she doesn't know who we're looking for. I mean, a person gets buried where they want to, not where the lady with the wheelbarrow thinks they should be buried."

However, he continued on, letting himself be led in the wrong direction, though he knew Jung was buried on the hill. But we'll go to this other cemetery first and look at every stone and then come back and climb the hill to the old cemetery. If we get there in the dark it doesn't matter.

They came to the newspaper office again. "Let me check the map one more time." He went inside, found Lake Zurich at the bottom of the map and realized he'd been looking at it upside down, in the manner of a true path finder. The cemetery should be right around the corner.

"I think it's that way," said Marie, "by the church we went to at the start."

They crossed over the stone bridge again, past the little stream, walked one block and saw the green lawn dotted with headstones. It was a small cemetery, surrounded by business and residential streets. "I'm sure the Warlock of Zurich's not buried here. There's too much noise all around—no communion with nature."

"We should look anyway."

"Sure," said DuJohn. "We've got to." He started at the extreme corner and began a methodical examination of each stone. He looked up and saw Marie wandering casually down the gravel lane. That was not the way to look, of course, but he didn't want to seem overbearing. He'd keep his mouth shut, look at every single stone himself, and in that way be absolutely certain Jung wasn't there.

He completed the first row, began on the second, studying each name carefully. A systematic approach is sometimes necessary, if uncertainty is not to creep in and take over one's mood. We've got that high hill to climb to the old cemetery and we want to be absolutely sure we're on the right trail, in order to open ourselves and flow with the undercurrent of the day. Jung is up there, where the view is, where the wind blows, where the old Swiss are buried.

Marie's whistle came to him, from behind a row of trees. As he turned the corner of the leaves, he saw her kneeling, placing the orchid into the earth, among other flowers. A small stone pool of water graced the edge of the grave.

So this is it, thought DuJohn, kneeling to read the gravestone:

Called or not, God is always present

Star Cruisers, Welcome

The ramp touched down in stone and rubble, and captain and crew descended. Here on the abandoned fringes of the city, they could move with impunity. On all sides were dilapidated buildings—windows broken, doors hanging off their hinges. A navigational assistant spoke over his map. "The inhabitants call it the Bronx."

"A wretched place—"

"Its degenerate quality, sir, is typical of all areas adjacent to the planet's civilized centers."

The captain turned back toward his spacecraft and was reassured by its hum of vigilance. Surrounding it were bands of vibrating light which none could approach without triggering annihilation. Its landing struts balanced it in a vacant lot between two dark buildings in a desolate landscape. No life moved, up and down deserted streets, and he anticipated no intrusion; should there be one, the ship could take care of itself.

"Will the inhabitants be of any practical use?"

"Something like pack animals, I suppose."

"You expect no resistance?"

"The creatures are retarded. There'll be some token fighting, but after a bout or two, they'll give in, I promise you."

The robot guard flanked the expeditionary group, and the party went forward. Doorways were investigated, found empty. Every building was abandoned. "The fleet can land here, as we thought. Conquest of Manhattan should take no more than an hour. The entire planet shall fall in similar fashion." The colonel's brilliant eyes glowed as they swept the landscape. "We'll level this area and Doctor 5's group will begin their cycling. The stone will be delicious, I'm told." The colonel's mouth made a loud grinding sound, and the captain's mouth repeated the feeding reflex with an ominous echo.

"Hungry?" quipped Doctor 5. "We'll eat soon enough. This whole altar of forgotten nourishment will be devoured. What creatures, not to have savored their finest delicacy, the planetary body itself."

"They eat only its by-products, sir," said an assistant. "That is their evolutionary path. It creates no strength, but it does leave the planet intact, while we have devoured ours and a good many others."

"We are titans of hunger," said the colonel. "That is our greatness."

The captain looked at the colonel and smiled at the old

soldier's mindless repetition of the army line. A little stale, perhaps? But where would we be without them, when there are worlds to be eaten?

The doctor and his team dug in the pockmarked street, whirling to great depths in seconds and bringing up layered samples. Analysis was performed and Doctor 5 nodded as each specimen was graded. "All quite satisfactory. We can digest the planet to the center, even here in this wasteland, this Bronx."

"Caution." The electronic voice of the robot guard sounded, and the machine sped forward. The captain moved up beside the guard. "What is it?"

"There." The robot's arm extended, toward a dark alleyway between two buildings. The captain sent the robot down it first, and then the group followed.

"What's he picking up?"

"I think he's oversensitized. I'm not getting anything from the environment, are you?"

"Probably the local rodent. Not much to worry about. Overly cautious, these mechanical monsters of ours." The doctor slapped the robot on the back.

"Caution." The robot repeated its observation, its electronic eyes illuminating a section of wall, on which large sprawling letters had been painted:

WALTON AVENUE BALDIES

"What could that mean? Bring the squawk box."

The sprawling letters of the message were copied into a small pulsing instrument, which received them with an internal whisper, clicked several times, and addressed the group. *"Walton . . . Avenue . . . thoroughfare in suggested Landing Area."* The machine paused, clicked again, continued. *"Bald—ies. Hairless beings? Need additional input."*

"No need for that," said the doctor. "Unimportant rubbish, like everything in this place. Switch it off."

The expeditionary party turned and withdrew from the dank corridor. "That glow in the sky ahead. That is the great city of Manhattan?"

"Easily surrounded by air and water. It'll be totally cut off, while our main garrison sets up here, in the more spacious if somewhat revolting Bronx."

The team started back up the darkened streets, toward the landing site, moving uninhibitedly now, through the desolate place. "Robot 2, continue forward there, no shuffling."

The robot's firing arm came up. *"Enemy attack."* The chilling mechanical indifference of its voice ran through the captain's brain, and he hurried forward, waves of alarm tingling through his mental coils. Then, turning the corner where the robot stood, he saw a sight he'd never thought to see in a thousand years' traveling of the galaxy.

"Impossible! It can't be—" He stood, ashen-faced, trembling, despair filling his soul. In another moment Colonel 12 was beside him. "What—"

"The ship . . ."

It stood before them in the moonlight, its hull stripped. The landing struts, wheels, brakes, were gone, and the ship had been tipped on its side like a beached whale. Its armor plate, capable of withstanding atomic attack, had somehow been pried off, leaving only a thin shell over the frame. The power hatches were open and the ship's primary guidance systems were hanging out in a tangle.

Rockets were gone, along with bomb loads. Even the portholes and cockpit windows had been dismantled, sockets gaping blindly at the sky.

The captain raced up the steps into the ship. A ruined interior awaited him, walls torn open, wires ripped out. He stumbled forward. The finest cruiser in the galaxy, reduced to junk inside an hour.

On all sides was destruction, every piece of hardware removed, including door latches. He stepped through into his command center. It lay in pieces before him, the brain of the ship lobotomized, cut, torn out, clipped off. He went to an automatic recording device, one of the few units left untouched. He pressed it, and the machine clicked on, replaying the sounds of the last hour.

"That's all the copper wire. Ought to bring five, ten dollar . . ."

". . . nice move, Benny. Fernando, get the chrome, an' those headphones . . ."

". . . Larry, grab that tv screen . . . and those revolvin' chairs . . "

". . . the whole fancy-pants burglar alarm system. Should be able to sell that somewhere . . ."

"Hey, you dudes done in there? We foun' the booze."

"Tha's some weird-smellin' juice. Sure it ain't hair oil?"

"Gonna drink it anyway . . ."

The captain switched the recorder off and stumbled his way back into the corridor. Colonel 12 was standing there amidst the wreckage. "... a miscalculation ... our reconnaissance ... nothing like this was reported ..."

"Reconnaissance," muttered the captain, looking at his dismantled cabin. His personal possessions were gone—his sun cups, his store of the wines of Canopus, other treasures gathered from around the universe. "They've ruined us, Colonel. In less than an hour."

The colonel stared from the doorway. "Some kind of scavenger—"

"Slightly more than that, Colonel. They disarmed a star cruiser. The finest security system in space was breached."

"They'll harass the fleet into its grave. They'll pick us bare."

"Quite," said the captain, and went back along the corridor, to the reserve power unit, where his Second had already begun a check. "They overlooked it, sir."

"Can we fly?"

"We can make rendezvous, Captain, that's about all. Then we shall have to transfer. The ship is lost."

The captain rubbed his face wearily, calculating the magnitude of such a loss. Their ships were life to them; nomads could have it no other way. He turned, as the colonel came into the room behind him. "Radio your command, Colonel. Inform them that we've learned the single most important fact about this planet."

"And what is that?"

"That it isn't worth it." The captain sent the expeditionary team to their emergency stations and took his position at the controls of the secondary unit. The torn, hanging hatches were pulled shut. The engines fired and the tilted ship righted itself. A second blast lifted it wobbling into the air, and like a tattered turban it rose slowly over the Bronx.

The ship pivoted precariously above the dark cityscape, in the direction of its rendezvous, a radio message already seeking out the distant mother ship that awaited them.

"*. . . disastrous encounter . . . ship nearly destroyed . . . request immediate assistance . . .*"

The beaten battle wagon accelerated upward, hull shaking loudly. Written upon it in pastel spray paint was an inscription:

THE BALDIES

With a violent shudder the ship, and its inscription, faded into the farther reaches of the night sky.

That Winter
When Prince Borisov
Was Everybody's
Favorite

The courtiers of the palace of Empress Anna Ivanovna conceived a wonderful plan—the erecting of a palace of ice. The Empress, bored by an especially long winter, thought it a splendid project. Workmen were brought from all over St. Petersburg and its outlying districts.

A large open field on the edge of the city was chosen for the building site. Blocks of snow were formed from the drifts there, and blocks of ice were hewn from the river and carried to the field. The ladies and gentlemen of the court came each day to watch the marvelous fancy take shape. They did not stay long, for the cold was severe. Only workmen continually on the move were able to spend the day there.

The ice palace rose up daily, one wall of blocks atop

another. When completed it was a small but striking edifice, a miniature gem of sparkling brilliance, caught by the distant January sun.

"Princess Kutisi, you must come inside," called Prince Borisov, the young man who first thought of the marvelous palace, and who had contributed most of the money for its construction.

The sun beamed through the windows and the translucent walls were glowing. Princess Kutisi skipped through the fairy-palace, streams of mist leaving her delicate nose and mouth. "How delightful," she said, whirling in her furs like a fairy-princess. The court was usually so dull. They were indebted to Prince Borisov for his extraordinary idea. "But it's awfully bare," she said after touring the rooms.

Prince Borisov rose to the occasion, glowing like the luminous interior of his palace. "We shall have furniture—of ice!"

The German cabinetmaker, Herr Oberhaffen, and his assistant, Brummer, were given the task of furnishing the ice palace.

"Beautiful," said young Brummer, entering the frozen building.

"The Russian brain," said Herr Oberhaffen, later, when they were alone, shaping the chair legs of ice, "shrinks in the cold weather."

Wing chairs, divans, and tables were constructed, and a magnificent bed. Young Brummer shaped the four posts of the bed in the form of nymphs. Herr Oberhaffen remarked that French blood must have tragically inserted itself somewhere in Brummer's ancestry, but the young man continued to shape figures into the headboard, elves and fairies of ice cavorting above the snow pillows.

Princess Kutisi and the other young women of the court fluttered around the furnished palace, testing the new chairs, but not for long. They certainly did not want to get rheumatism in their lovely hips.

"In summer we shall build a palace beneath the sea, eh?" said the old German as he took the handsome purse of his wages from Prince Borisov.

"Why, yes. What an idea!" exclaimed the Prince, and young Brummer was already decorating in his imagination the undersea bedroom, with mermaids bearing shells of plenty, their tails curled around the bedposts.

"What a pity that no one lives here," said Princess Kutisi, when she and the Prince were once again outside, beneath the gleaming walls of ice, which had been sprayed with water to solidify the seams.

"Well, then, someone shall live here," said Prince Borisov.

That night the throne room of the Empress was filled with a strange topic—the marriage feast next day of two serfs; but it was no ordinary marriage and Empress Anna remarked to the Prince that it was charming of him to have given the young couple the ice palace to live in.

The couple was a clownish pair—Yar Passock, stableboy of Prince Borisov, and Katris, a servant girl from the retinue of Princess Kutisi. In clothes of great splendor, such as they had never worn, nor ever dreamed of wearing—a brocade suit and cape for the stableboy, a gown of fine, intricate lace for the servant girl—the couple was led to the altar of the cathedral of St. Petersburg, and with the entire court of the Empress Anna Ivanovna in attendance, they were solemnly wed by a patriarch of the Church.

Court gossip was that this peasant union was but the shadow of an impending marriage between Prince Borisov and Princess Kutisi, and so all were in an intoxicated mood when the newlyweds were carried in gilded coach, seated on silk cushions, to their marriage palace, which stood glistening in the moonlight.

"Oh, Yar," said the excited servant girl as they drew near, "it is so thrilling."

"Yes," said the stableboy, "our master and mistress believe in sharing good things."

"We are very lucky," said Katris, cuddling next to her husband. What strange fate to have been cast up so high, so suddenly, when but a day ago she was carrying hot water to her mistress's bath. Now I am a mistress myself, of a palace! Who would have dreamed that the place which had been the center of every eye in St. Petersburg for a month would be hers!

The coach stopped. The stableboy opened the door, helping his wife down the steps, taking care she did not stumble in her vast, unfamiliar gown.

"My boy," called the coachman, old Fonviz, who'd taught young Passock all he knew about horses.

Passock answered with only half-attention, for drawing near were the coaches of all the courtiers of the Empress, blazing with lamps, loud with voices.

"This place—" said the coachman, pointing with his whip to the fairy-palace, but the stableboy was not listening. Prince Borisov was beside him, filled with merriment, placing his hand on the boy's shoulder, as one gentleman to another.

"Such a night as this brings many rewards," said the Prince as they walked toward the silver-shining doorway. "First, you have won the greatest treasure—" He bowed his head toward the bride, who glowed with warmth beneath her white fur wraps. "And to it has been added your freedom, my son," said the Prince in a fatherly tone, though he was not much older than his stableboy. "I have arranged for this field, on which your palace sits, to become rightfully yours at dawn. When summer comes you might wish to begin blacksmith work, and I shall see to it you have a few gold pieces to start you off."

"My Prince," said the stableboy, his eyes brimming with tears.

"Well, now, look sharp, the Empress has come!" The Prince and his blissful couple turned in the doorway, toward the clatter of royal hoofbeats, as the coach of the sovereign came down the road, between the rows of halted carriages, and itself halted, directly in front of the ice palace of Yar Passock.

The door of the carriage opened. The Empress placed her foot on its step.

"All hail!" cried Prince Borisov, and a cheer from the courtiers set the mood of the evening, of rollicking fun.

The tables of ice were loaded with food, and lamps were hung in every room, turning the walls of ice into magic shadow-shows. When the music began, the Empress enjoyed a waltz, but her feet grew too cold to finish and she left the dance floor to the more youthful revelers, whose fiery spirit could not be chilled, and of these Yar Passock and his wife, Katris of the snow-white veil, were most indefatigable, for they were free—free as the wind!

Princess Kutisi was unusually lovely that evening, in lengths of wild furs, her cheeks glowing, her shoes skipping over the ice floor as she waltzed with Prince Borisov, himself as striking as an emperor, possessing the tall, strong figure of his family, high cheekbones, dark, flashing eyes. And this night was his doing—a colorful celebration indeed. All knew he was the favorite of the Empress this winter, and a gift of some desirable acreage would be his, no doubt, with a fine palace upon it.

"To the bride!" cried Prince Borisov at midnight, leading the salute.

"To the groom!" Princess Kutisi signaled the final fanfare of the evening, and the last dance was played. The bride and groom waltzed alone, like a fairy-king and -queen, in their enchanted domain. The dance ended, Yar Passock bowed to his former chief, Prince Borisov, and stood at the doorway of the palace with his wife as his guests departed, one by one, the most noble faces in Petersburg, his guests!

The noise of the carriages diminished, the laughter faded, until there was only the wind, blowing through the cracks in the door and through the shutters of the windows. The couple went to the kitchen, where piles of food still remained on the tables. Yar Passock selected a finger of sausage and put it to his lips.

"Frozen already," he said with a laugh, putting it back. "Well, it will keep all the better."

"I'm cold," said Katris, "now that everyone has gone."

"Why, then, we shall cover you with furs," said the lord of the frozen manor, and he led his wife to their bedroom, and the bed of ice, on which lay a pile of fine furs. "You just slip into these," said the new husband solicitously, "and I shall bring all the lamps into this room. They shall throw a good heat."

The girl crawled into the pile of furs, and curled herself into a tight ball. It was all so strange, like a story she'd heard as a child, but could not quite remember, about a princess, and something dreadful, but it turned out all right in the end. It always did.

Yar Passock entered with a string of lanterns in each hand, which he placed on ice tables at either side of the bed, so that the bedroom was lit up like a throne room, and the nymphs on the bedposts danced in the flickering light.

Katris curled herself deeper in the covers. "Please come now," she said, "and hold me."

"Yes," said Yar Passock, "yes, dear wife." He had drunk much wine, and he had warmth enough for both of them, warmth and plenty, a little shop of his own in springtime.

"Hold me," she begged, shivering.

He held her, intimately as he could through their many furs. Katris was in there somewhere, her soft body his very own, for the taking, for the keeping.

"Just hold me," she said.

"Yes," he said. "We'll warm up soon. One gets used to the cold. The blood thickens. All will be fine. Tomorrow we are free, and many stories will be told about us after this night, you'll see. I wager we will enjoy the inside of the Empress's palace. Yes, I'm certain of it!"

She felt warmer now that he was here. Such a strange wedding day, hard to believe, like a fairy tale. It was right on the edge of her memory, the princess goes to live with a young prince, but his castle is haunted—was that it? She could almost see the gay princess dancing. Grandmother had told her that story. I am so tired from all my dancing. And then she was asleep and dreamt the story and it did turn out fine in the end and they danced round and round.

Yar Passock's own dream was of a splendor fitting for a man who has just gained his freedom. He and his wife were taken to the palace of the Empress. It was more fantastic than he'd imagined, with enormous ceilings, gold everywhere, tremendous music, and the Empress herself, radiant as an icon, was seated on her throne. How strange it should be made of ice, and her face was that of his own wife, Katris!

Prince Borisov and Princess Kutisi were the first of the courtiers to arrive next morning, after late breakfast. They were horribly surprised to find Yar Passock and his wife frozen in the embrace of death, and it was a whole day before the bodies were thawed enough to separate into different caskets.

In spite of this unusual end to the celebrated marriage, Prince Borisov received, as everyone had predicted, a large tract of land from the Empress, with a lovely summer palace on it, overlooking the sea. Plans for an undersea palace were discussed, but set aside for lack of experienced divers.

Fana

Al-nujum attached himself to a caravan, for he'd been alone long enough beneath the silent orbit of the stars. Now once again he might enjoy the voices of other drivers in the night.

Zahir, owner of the caravan, was an old acquaintance, whose throat Al-nujum had saved during an attack by the bandit known as Uncomfortable Hump. Al-nujum had crossed weapons with Uncomfortable Hump and smiled into the bandit's filthy beard, which smelled so bad men often gagged in its presence. Zahir was thus ever ready to employ Al-nujum and to receive him into his tent, as he did now, at evening, calling for khalifati sweets and wine to be placed before himself and his guest.

"What piece of the Divine Plan, praise be its subtlety, have you discerned since last we met?" Smiling, the merchant extended the dish of sweetmeats to his favored employee.

"Nothing of consequence and yet—"

"Speak, swordsman, your voice cannot utter the inconsequential."

"I've seen no one through months of wandering, speaking only to myself and my steed, and perhaps I have lost touch with what is real—"

"It is there one meets the First Angel of God."

"Angel or devil, I do not know," said Al-nujum. "In any case, I have not been quite myself, and on the day of which I shall tell, perhaps I drank more than is wise—"

"Our life is a lonely one, and the path is ever shifting."

"I came to the three lakes of Uau-en-Namus, whose waters of blue, green, and red are the eyes of Allah, all homage to his beauty."

"Indeed, we can only stand in awe before it, et cetera," nodded Zahir.

"As I gazed at the waters of the red pool, an apparition rose before me, of a dancing girl, the loveliest of creatures. I watched her dance and forgot all weariness, self-doubt, and pain. But—" Al-nujum paused, sighing. "—she was a mirage, and I was left with nothing but water in my hands."

"Yes," said the merchant, "life is full of fading delights. I myself have spent the past year seeking a temple in the dunes. In my dreams I open it and find within, nestled upon a cushion of red velvet, a snake coiled around an enormous jewel. I steal the snake and leave the jewel. As for dancing girls, I have one with me, the most exquisite either of us has ever seen. I am selling her to

Sultan Mahid-din, he-who-abolishes-religion, cursed be his name."

"And who is this dancing girl?"

"She is called Fana." The merchant signaled to the servant boy, then turned back to Al-nujum. "The Sultan, may he be overcharged in the bargain, has already given me a substantial down payment, but I myself paid a handsome price for this Moorish beauty, and she is said to possess talents other than the dance." Old Zahir sighed, for in the past year he had lost the ability to perform at love, and the loss weighed heavily on his soul.

"The musicians, master." The servant boy held the tent flap for three troubadors who bore with them a three-hosed hookah of shining brass. Of the tribe called Veiled Men of the Sahara, their white face cloth would be lifted only to admit the mouthpiece of the hookah to their faintly smiling lips.

While the musicians tuned their instruments, Al-nujum relaxed upon silken pillows, beneath tent walls embroidered with stars. And then, from outside the tent, he heard the sound of ankle bells.

Fana entered, and Al-nujum rose with a start from his pillow. The adorable creature was the dancing girl of the mirage of Uau-en-Namus! She had risen from the waters of the red lake at morning and her dancing was, he'd thought, a dream. Now, as she came closer and her thin silken pants whispered at her hips, now, in the tent of his friend, Zahir—is Al-nujum still dreaming?

The old merchant leaned toward Al-nujum. "There is a certain bird, have you heard its song? They say a man may listen for a moment only."

Her hair was shining black, decorated with a band of small sapphires which fastened behind her ears, holding there the knots of her veil, a thin seven-colored fabric through which her lips could be seen, and on them was a smile of aloofness, as if the men before her were the slaves, and not she.

"They have these airs," Zahir said in a delighted whisper, and reached for another ripe fig bursting from its skin like Fana from her immodest costume.

She stood in the hushed moment before the downbeat of the drum, hand on her hip, the hip jutted out in languid indolence. The drum sounded, joined by flute and twanging strings, and the slave girl began the dance called Secret.

Exquisitely obscene movements rippled her body, and the jewel in her navel winked at Al-nujum. He stared, fascinated, then discovered his teeth were chattering. She turned, hips swiveling hypnotically, and Al-nujum's body trembled, from a sorcery he could not comprehend; he was no child, he'd seen women dance before. But a goddess had entered Fana. Her profile astonished him, so perfect was its beauty, the eyes holding an understanding no man's mind could compass. He sank into her magic, and ecstasy filled him. *You are a sorceress,* he whispered. *I am a dancer,* she replied, and her dance carried her past him.

She circled the tent, and then turned slowly to Zahir, who had watched with amusement as the girl had devastated his dear friend, Al-nujum. Now the slave girl thinks to enslave me.

The old merchant stroked his beard and sighed as Fana undulated before him, for he was too old to erect the tent-pole ever again, cursed be his misfortune. Why, o Lord, have you given your faithful servant such a brief time of joy?

He saw clearly through her silken costume to the smoothness of her young limbs, and felt a dreadful ache in his temples. His heart made no sense, his eardrums were pounding, may God protect me from a stroke. He waved her off with a limp gesture, but Fana remained, and through the billow of her silken pants he saw far too much, and heard women groaning somewhere in his head, deep groans of desire sounding, as if some hero of the desert were tormenting them with his prowess. And Zahir remembered, and knew from whence these memories came, remembered that he himself had once been that hero.

The old man wiped his brow. Really, this is too much. My forehead is perspiring; my pulse has quickened to a frantic rhythm; my old tent-pole—*has risen as of old?*

There is no God but Allah!

He had paid a fortune to astrologers, soothsayers, and potion-sellers, with never a sign of the great stiffening. But this simple girl—

Old Zahir luxuriated in her dance now, for tonight would be a marvelous adventure. When the dance is done, she and I will retire to coition, Allah watch over my blood pressure. He turned to Al-nujum. "I am delivered, my friend. The night is mine once more."

But Al-nujum did not hear; the lonely camel driver

was rising from his cushion. Fana would be his and no one else's. There is none but Fana!

Old Zahir saw, as if in a dream, his friend Al-nujum draw his sword, and knew—it was for Fana. He rose and drew his own sword, a sudden fury in his limbs. He would not be cheated, not now, when his youth had been returned to him. And then as their weapons crossed with a clang, old Zahir had a terrible realization—that his friend was the better swordsman. This blade that passes through my ribs, piercing my heart's chamber, this pain, this curse coming to me on the very night I have erected the old tent-pole again—I have always known it would turn out like this, for . . . I once overcharged . . . an . . . old woman.

The veiled musicians scrambled toward the tent door, only to die at Al-nujum's maddened hand, their spirits rising to the Blue Mountains of Heaven where their ancestral tribe is encamped. Fana watched, amused, as one who is beyond the reach of good and evil.

Al-nujum carried her away, down the great avenues of the dunes, and all around them, stirred by the winds, sand devils danced. At dawn they reached one of the most terrible spots on earth, that place known as the Devil's Garden, where the wind forms columns of sandstone and chalk, shaping them into objects resembling houses and huts, in which no sane man would ever seek to rest—and there Al-nujum rested.

Fana sat quietly in the doorway of one of the dream-twisted chalk houses, her thin costume touched by a gentle morning breeze. Al-nujum secured the camels and then came to her, and with bloodstained fingers caressed his prize. For this he would have slain the Angel of God himself. As Fana's costume fell to the sand, as she returned his caress with her own, Al-nujum experienced the supernatural tumescence called *el-hammache,* the camel whip. He applied it according to tradition, and even Fana, goddess of love, groaned in the sand.

Al-nujum saw a thousand goddesses within him, bearing the substance of creation in cups of ivory, over which it spilled, jeweled and sparkling. *"Fana,"* he whispered, and she plunged him deeper into the mystery of being, opening the portal of his heart. There waited a white camel bearing a noble sheik. In the hoofbeats of the camel Al-nujum heard the drumming of time, and in the eyes of the sheik he saw the race of man. The sheik's own heart was a flame which no man could extinguish, and here Al-nujum was inclined to rest—but Fana undulated once more.

He tossed upon her, and felt the earth, its wholeness and extension bearing every dream and flower, all beasts, gems, dragons, religions. *All that humanity has done was done by me,* explained the higher voice, within whose occult tone Al-nujum sought now to remain—but Fana pressed her thighs to his, and raised him higher.

His brain opened its guarded rooms, those reserved for vision of the shadow of God, and there Al-nujum saw the nature of the sun, secret of life beyond word and song.

Later, when his passion had been spent, and his illumination was fading, the grains of sand in Fana's hair still sparkled for him with solar force. He would rest now, and reflect, for he knew the Secret.

"There is yet another veil before one passes through to Allah," she said.

"And will you remove that veil for Al-nujum your slave?"

"It requires an offering," she said.

"I can but offer my life," said the camel driver.

"You may have to. Sultan Mahid-din has a claim on me. As long as he lives, some force will draw me to him, and he will confine me."

They rode to the city of the sultan, and Al-nujum left Fana in the marketplace at nightfall. He slipped past one hundred warriors of the sultan, and entered the palace gates, for he was one who held the charm of love, which, while it burns, lends men grace. Ascending a balcony of gold, he entered the sultan's bedchamber and smothered the royal sleeper with a white silken pillow.

Still protected by love, he escaped unseen and rejoined Fana in the marketplace. On the Street of the Carpet Beaters, they enjoyed rice with sesame paste. "The offering has been made," he said, giving her the dead sultan's ring.

"The last knot is violent undoing," said Fana. "Are you sure you wish it?"

"There is a certain bird, do you know its song?"

"Very well," said Fana, and touched his brow lightly with her fingertip. The restaurant walls dissolved before Al-nujum's eyes, as did the city, the sands, the world. Then slowly, he began to perceive the stars of another world, soft and mellow, on a sky of dark blue cloth. *"In*

Fana

this way are sins erased," said Fana's voice, and he saw
that the sky was a tent, and the stars upon it were sewn of
luminous thread, and this tent was Zahir's, and he and
Zahir were sprawled on cushions, and Fana was dancing
before them. The old merchant was leaning toward him
saying, "I just had the most astonishing vision, that you
had killed me, dear friend." He took Al-nujum's hand.
"You must forgive my dark thought. I am nervous,
for tonight, very soon, when her dance is done—*el-
hammache!"* Then, as if troubled by another dark
thought, as if the vision of Al-nujum's violence were still
attending him, he turned to his friend once more and
said, "She is young and wild. Perhaps you would care to
tame her a little for me first, my friend. Go, take her, and
I will enter later when she is quieter and less liable to give
me heart failure."

Al-nujum made his apologies, and when the dance was
ended he withdrew and mounted his camel. As the musicians left the tent he heard the drummer say, "We smoke
too much kif. I had a vision that we were murdered by
the driver."

"One can never smoke too much kif," said the flute
player.

"Perhaps you are right," said the drummer.

Al-nujum urged his camel forward, across the star-
shaped dunes where he resumed his lonely wandering.

*   *   *

Old Zahir, filled with new life and happiness, brought
his caravan to the city of Sultan Mahid-din. Zahir's
course was clear, he must refund the sultan's down pay-

ment on Fana, for he would not part with the girl now, not for all the sultan's wealth. However, it was learned that no such refund was necessary, for the sultan had died peacefully, in his sleep. A white bird had been found on his chest that morning, speaking the single word, *Fana.*

Rejoicing over his good fortune, old Zahir returned to his camp to inform Fana of the great saving he'd made, a small fortune which he would give her as their wedding present.

"She has gone, master," said the flute player, who was sitting on the sand, cleaning his instrument.

Old Zahir felt himself growing white as the bird who could only speak the single word, *Fana.*

"She went off with the drummer. The pig took our three-hosed hookah as well, and a tremendous quantity of kif."

"In trade," said old Zahir, sadly staring out across the trackless sands, "many treasures pass through a merchant's hands."